GHOST WRITER

Haunted Everly After

BOOK NINE

REGINA WELLING
ERIN LYNN

Ghost Writer

ISBN- 978-1-953044-65-5

Cover design by: L. Vryhof

Interior design by: L. Vryhof

http://reginawelling.com

http://erinlynnwrites.com

First Edition

Printed in the U.S.A.

Contents

CHAPTER ONE

"Score first, stripper second," Patrea warned in case I was doing it wrong.

"Are we talking about the wallpaper or my love life?" I couldn't help teasing, then laughed when she rolled her eyes at me.

"If you have to ask," she teased back, "you're probably missing the point somewhere."

We didn't talk about why I'd been spending so much time helping her with her house-flipping project. She knew I needed the distraction from my falling out with

Neena. Also, there was something oddly satisfying about peeling back the layers of old paper to reveal each successive pattern underneath.

Interesting layers so far on this wall. One with pink and white stripes, the next a bunch of chocolate blobs riding across a background of harvest gold—utterly seventies. Under that, splashy pink cabbage roses strewn across a field of dark blue, and the most difficult so far, also pink and stripey, but sprinkled with yellow flowers that never existed in nature.

"It's coming off okay? And you're not overdoing it with your wrist?" Covered in a fine layer of plaster dust and wearing a pair of faded overalls, her hair bundled under a scarf and her eyes wrapped with a set of protective goggles, Patrea put down the pry bar she'd been using and came to check on me.

This DIY warrior looked nothing like the put-together, slightly stuffy attorney who'd helped me during the first days of my divorce. The current version seemed looser, happier, and far more animated. With a new husband and a big move in her recent past, Patrea had come a long way since the day she'd turned up on my doorstep the Christmas before. She'd settled into small-town living like she'd been born to it. I liked to think I had something to do with the changes.

"So far, but it's a lot of layers." Five, to be exact. I pointed toward the section where I'd made the most progress. "And my wrist is fine. Doesn't even hurt anymore. But should there be cloth underneath the paper? And should it be crunchy?"

Going in for a closer look, Patrea nodded. "That's an old sheet and was probably applied using homemade wheat paste. You can tell by the color as it ages."

"Wheat paste?"

"Flour, sugar, and water, basically. Boiled together, they form a thick glue."

"Huh. You learn something new every day," I said as my phone beeped to signal an incoming text.

"Jacy?" Patrea questioned when I checked to see who it was from, and I shook my head.

It wasn't that my oldest friend, Jacy, had chosen her business partner over me when Neena decided she couldn't handle my ability to see ghosts; that wasn't Jacy's way. I had been the one to pull back because I didn't want to put her in the middle of a problem that had nothing to do with her.

"It's Delilah Cannon."

"Who?" With tender care, Patrea pried off a length of baseboard, crowed with pleasure when it came off intact.

"Davina Benet's former doppelganger."

Flipping the board over, Patrea tapped her hammer against a nail to push it back through the front far enough to grab with the forked end of the prybar. "Davina had a doppelganger? How did I not hear about this before?"

I remembered why. "She popped up here at Halloween when you were in, you know." I flipped my hand to keep from saying the word jail. Plus, now that Patrea knew about my ghost issues, I could tell her the entire story, which I did.

"You should have seen the look on Martha's face when Davina got all spookified and busted up her little publicity stunt. I know it's not nice to laugh at people's misfortune, and you know I appreciate everything Martha has done for me, but I made an exception because she totally brought that comeuppance on herself."

While Patrea laughed along with me, I could practically see the questions dancing around in her head, but the only one she let out was, "Why's this Delilah person texting you now?" She nodded toward the phone I still held in my left hand.

I glanced at the screen to double-check my facts.

"She says she's writing a book about Davina."

Patrea's brows shot up. "Really?" She drew the word out long.

"A tell-all, she says. And she's asked me to find her a place to stay in Mooselick River so she can be closer to Davina's spirit while she works on it."

"Davina's spirit? Does that mean what I think it means?"

"No," I shook my head. "She doesn't have a clue Davina's still hanging around here."

"Okay, so this should be interesting."

"You have no idea." I sent a text back saying I'd look into it for her and followed up with a request for the timing of her plans. "Delilah was Davina's biggest fan, but the admiration was a one-way thing."

I put my phone away and went back to stripping wallpaper while Patrea finished pulling nails, slashed a number three on the back of the baseboard, and stacked it with the rest. "You're numbering them because you plan to put them back?"

Nodding, Patrea moved on to the next. "Yes, that's right, but back to Delilah. I'm fascinated by this book-writing plan. I wonder what Davina will think of it."

"That's the million-dollar question, and I haven't got a clue what the answer will be. I haven't seen much of Davina since the night we took Martin Walker down. In a way, I find that worrisome."

A short silence followed before Patrea said, "Why?"

I shrugged. "She got way into helping Jober cross over, which did not turn out so well for me. And then, that same day you dragged me out of the house, she popped back up asking for my help with another spirit she ran into, but I couldn't help because of how my ghost thing works."

"Explain, please." Fascinated, Patrea gave me her full attention.

"Not much to tell, really. I consulted a psychic, and according to her, Leandra's meddling opened some kind of psychic door or something and probably set up some ridiculous beacon that lets spirits on this side of the veil find and haunt me."

As usual, Patrea clued in when it came to the nuances. Head tilted, she gave me an up-and-down look. "Why are they on this side of the veil? And what does that make you? A medium or a sensitive? Clairvoyant? Is there a difference?"

Shrugging, I said, "According to Kat—that's the medium's name—a true medium can speak to those who have passed behind or beyond the veil. It's an active talent, while mine is more passive. I'm limited to those who are stuck on this side. Like with unfinished business, or whatever. I don't think there's a name for it. I'm haunted."

Patrea mirrored my shrug. "Okay. I guess I see the difference."

Nodding, I continued, "Anyhow, Davina wants to set up some ghost outreach program, and she wants me to help."

"Would that be so bad?"

Only if she decided to make it a lifelong— or rather a death-long—goal. One that would keep her on this side of the veil. In Mooselick River, and in my life.

"It wouldn't, but I have a selfish reason for wanting her to cross over." It felt good to talk about this stuff with someone like Patrea.

Despite her absolute acceptance of the esoteric, she was a logical thinker, and always gave thoughtful advice.

When I hesitated to share, she circled a hand to get me to continue. I sighed.

"What I'm about to tell you cannot leave this room, but my mother also has mediumistic tendencies, so part of my ability is inherent. I might have eventually come into my talent on my own, or I might not have. We'll never know because Momma Wade did her hoodoo on me and forced the issue."

"Hoodoo," Patrea repeated. "Good word."

"Right? I think she hexed me to find bodies, too. Makes me feel like a death magnet, but I have no proof that's the case."

Hammer and boards forgotten for the moment, Patrea dug in. "Tell me more. I'm fascinated."

"You've heard most of it," I shrugged. "Basically, I find the body; I see the ghost."

Except for that one time with the haunted pajamas, but even then, there was a tenuous connection between the girl who'd worn them and me. "So far, it's been just the ghosts of murdered people whose bodies I found, or in one case, didn't find, but was near the body shortly after the death."

"Because the spirit was just hanging around waiting for justice." Patrea proved she'd been listening. "And you don't see just any ghost, so you couldn't channel my dead grandmother and ask her where she hid her peach cobbler recipe."

"Not that I know of, but I'm sure Kat would be happy to handle that for you. I'll give you her number if you like."

"Later." For now, Patrea was more interested in my story than in connecting with her relatives. "Did she tell you anything else?"

"Not really. Once I help the dead find justice, they go into the light, and I never see them again, which is fine with me. Or some of them, anyway. Amber hung around awhile."

Patrea slugged me in the arm.

"Ow," I yelped, putting my other hand over the sore spot. "What was that for?"

"For holding out on me. Amber was in the house when I was there at Christmas, wasn't she?"

I nodded. "She had a lot of energy, that one. Used to give me the news every morning before I got out of bed. Complete with the weather report."

"Why didn't you say anything?"

A complicated question, but the answer I gave was simple. "I didn't want you to look at me like Neena did. Does."

"Fair enough, I guess." But I could tell she was hurt that I'd made an assumption about her.

"I'm sorry. If it helps, I wanted to tell you."

"But you didn't. You told Jacy, though, right?"

Oops, another minefield to navigate.

"Yes, but only under extreme circumstances." Because there was no reason not to, I told her how my attempt to help Spencer Charles cross over had put Jacy's life in danger. "And that's why I've been careful about what I say to anyone. I don't want my friends getting hurt on my account."

Patrea's voice went dry as dust. "How noble of you."

"Don't," I pleaded, close to tears. "You don't know what it's like."

"Don't I? I watched you nearly get choked to death by something that shouldn't have been able to touch you, and I couldn't do anything to stop it."

The memory shivered across my skin. "That's the first time anything like that has happened, and it wasn't on purpose. Davina believes that Jober's complete denial of his death caused something like the ghost version of a psychotic break. I think she's half right. He was already suffering from mental health issues after the death of his family and couldn't handle what happened, so he went over the edge."

"So that doesn't happen every time?"

Solemnly, I shook my head. "Never has before. Or not by a ghost. Hudson's killer tried to choke me to death, but he was just a human jerk. Hudson saved me by rolling one of Catherine's mannequin head down the stairs. Scored a perfect strike."

"Ghost bowling. There's a mental image I never thought I'd have."

"You and me both. I could die happy if people would leave my neck alone. For a second there, I thought I was a goner."

"You and me both, sister." Satisfied with my response, Patrea went back to pulling nails. "That's all very interesting, but you never said what's in it for you when Davina leaves."

"Well, you know that door Leandra opened? Davina thinks she can close it behind her when she goes."

After a short pause, Patrea asked the big question, "Does that mean you wouldn't see ghosts at all anymore?"

"That's her theory, and she knows about my mother and whatever got passed down through her to me, so I'm hoping Davina actually does know what she's talking about. Not that it matters if she decides not to cross over."

The prying of baseboards stopped. "They can choose to stay?"

"To a point, I guess. I'm no expert on ghostly shenanigans, but Amber didn't leave just because I'd found her killer. I had to make a deal with her to get her to move on. Saved my sanity when she finally went. Besides being my self-appointed news reporter, she lacked a sense of personal space."

I shuddered every time I even thought about the way ghost touches felt.

Patrea noticed my expression. "What's so bad about that?"

"Imagine if you washed the dirtiest, greasiest dishes ever to be used, then left your dishwater in the sink for a week. Nasty, right? With chunks of floating food and muck." Must have been because Patrea grimaced. "Then imagine you put that greasy, scummy mess in the refrigerator to get nice and cold before you dumped it down your back."

Now, it was Patrea's turn to shudder. "Okay, that would be slimy and disgusting."

"Add in the sensation of spiders crawling across your skin, and that's what it feels like to touch a ghost." Because even talking about it evoked the sensation, I shuddered again. "Amber preferred to ignore the rule about keeping her distance."

"There are rules?" Dropping the last baseboard on the pile, Patrea picked up a putty knife to help peel back the layers of wallpaper. "Who makes them?"

"Me. They're mine, and there are only three. No talking to me in public. Amber had trouble with that one, too. Another is that I don't give messages to loved ones. Most of the time, anyway, and they have to respect my personal space, which also includes staying out of my bedroom and bathroom."

Long sheets of paper fell under Patrea's knife. How did she do that? All I could seem to manage were a bunch of small shreds.

"Do you think the messages part is what Neena's having so much trouble with?" And now, Patrea got around to the most painful question. "You held out on her."

It felt like my stomach rolled over. "I gave her the message. I just didn't tell her it was directly from Hudson, but you're right. I held out on her, and I shouldn't have because it cost too much. Still, I'm not sure it's just about that with her. She reacted badly when Viola didn't understand Davina's talent and tried to get her to channel Hudson."

"Neena will come around," Patrea repeated what Jacy had said.

"I hope so, but I'm not counting on anything."

Wisely, Patrea changed the subject and showed me her trick for getting larger sections of wallpaper off at a time. Every so often, she'd give me a measuring look, and I couldn't tell if it had to do with the ghost thing or if she hoped I'd get inspired to do some remodeling of my own.

In the end, it turned out to be neither.

"Chris thinks we're ready to start a family."

I dropped my putty knife, then schooled the surprise out of my expression when I bent hastily to pick it up. "That's big news. What do you think?"

"You know I never expected to fall in love, and it happened so fast."

"Same with Drew and me, so I get it, but does that mean you don't want kids?"

Slowly, Patrea shook her head. "That's the thing. I think I do. I mean, like, I really think I do."

Excited, I nearly beaned her with the scoring tool when I pulled her in for a hug. "That's fantastic. Will you start trying right away? Maybe you and Jacy will be baby-buddies."

"Maybe. Or maybe you could put Drew out of his misery, marry the man, and we could all be baby-buddies together."

"I'm not sure the world is ready for that." If Patrea meant to tease, she missed the mark because I'd been thinking about my future with Drew a lot lately. "We haven't even had our first big fight yet. I think it might be too soon to consider this a forever thing."

Serious now, Patrea turned her full attention on me. "Don't."

"Don't what?"

"Don't measure Drew against what happened with Paul. You're not that young, inexperienced person anymore, and besides, Paul was a predator who knew exactly how to play you. Not because of who you were, but because he'd taken being a sleezebag to an art form. He and

Drew are night and day."

"In my heart, I know that's true. My head just doesn't want to catch up."

"Just because things happened fast both times, it doesn't mean your judgment is skewed."

How did she know exactly what I'd been worrying about?

"I guess not. My mother loves Drew, and she never liked Paul. As much as I hate to say it, I trust her judgment more than mine. But there's this other thing. He remembers the first time we met—in detail—while I barely noticed him. Maybe I should have felt something or remembered him more if we were meant to be like soul mates, or whatever."

Patrea snorted. "Or whatever. You're a piece of work, Everly Dupree. So what if you didn't remember meeting some boy for a day when you were just a girl? You love him now, and now is all that matters. Why haven't you had the big fight?"

I frowned. "I don't know."

"Yes, you do." Patrea wasn't having any of that excuse. "Think about it, and don't tell me it's because you agree on everything. If you say that, I will call you a liar, and I might also barf on your shoes. Nice boots, by the way."

We returned to scraping wallpaper while I considered the question, and finally came out with, "We don't agree on everything, but we don't argue. We debate. We discuss. And if we're both tired, we might snap a little at each other. But you can't argue with Drew because he's…I don't know exactly how to put it."

"A suck-up?" Patrea supplied helpfully. "Pushover. Under your thumb."

"No, and that's not very flattering because it makes him sound boring, and he's not. He's just Drew. He has a way of listening to what's under the words and understanding what's inside me. He has plenty of fire in him, but he doesn't turn it into anger and then dump it on the people he loves. He'd rather beat the hell out of a punching bag than argue over who should have unloaded the dishwasher."

"That's all well and good, but it also sucks."

"How do you figure?"

"Isn't it obvious? The lack of make-up sex. You're really missing out there."

My face flamed. Thank you, red hair and light skin. "If things got any better in that department, I'm not sure I could handle it."

"Okay, then." Patrea let the conversation die, but she allowed herself a smirk and got me thinking, which was probably the point.

CHAPTER TWO

"What's she doing back here?"

It was already chilly in the grocery store's produce section, so I didn't notice the familiar shiver from Davina Benet's ghostly presence until her voice sounded way too close to my ear.

"Who?" I pitched my voice low and turned away to keep anyone from seeing my mouth moving, but I already knew who she meant.

"Don't play dumb. Delilah Cannon is back in town, and I think you know something about it."

"Do I look like the tourist information center to you?"

Davina smirked and deliberately trailed a finger across a display of oranges, leaving a line of frost behind. "You know something."

"Cut it out. I'll have to pay for those now." I hissed from between clenched teeth. It's probably a good thing I was never tempted to go into ventriloquism since I'm pretty sure I'd be bad at it.

"Yes, I knew she was coming to town, but I didn't think she'd show up this soon. It has only been two days since she texted me to find her a place to stay. She's writing a book."

The next part required a deep breath before I said, "About you."

And since I figured I might as well get it all out in the open, I added, "A tell-all." Maybe the public nature of the conversation would keep the ghostly shenanigans to a minimum.

Davina snorted, and the air temperature returned to normal. Funny, I'd have thought that news would have the opposite effect on her. You just never know what might set someone off. Or not.

While I waited for Davina to chime in with her inevitable opinion, I put the formerly-frosted oranges in my cart. It was sort of my fault they got that way, and no one else should have to pay for blemished fruit.

"Fine by me," Davina finally said. "Just before I died, I inked a streaming deal for reruns of the show. That money goes into a college fund for my nieces and nephews, so if she wants to write a book that drums up publicity and makes the show more profitable, more power to her."

"You won't make trouble for Delilah, then?"

"When have I ever?" Davina winked in a way that sent dread through my veins and faded away.

"When have you ever not?" I muttered to no one and headed toward the checkout. "And don't help me figure out who killed you, either."

I may have said that last bit at a higher volume than I intended because I got a weird look from the woman who'd just come by to pick out a head of lettuce.

"Sorry, I'm in a play. Just practicing my lines." The lie turned my face hot and red.

The woman nodded, but in that way a person does when they're humoring someone who's clearly not entirely with themselves. Since I couldn't see any avenue for redemption, I let her think whatever she wanted and managed to get back to my car just as Neena Montayne pulled into the parking lot.

She saw my car, and she saw me, but looked right through me as if she didn't. "Just jab the knife in a little deeper, why don't you?"

It hurt to lose a friend because of the one part of my life I had no control over. People are more than just one thing. They are more than what they do for a living. They are more than what political party they belong to. They are more than whatever role they play in family or society, and yet, we are often judged by these singular aspects. It was disheartening to realize that every other good quality I possess couldn't balance out the one thing about me that freaked Neena out. That nothing I could do would matter as much to her as seeing ghosts.

Sure, it was her problem and her loss, but knowing that didn't make me feel one whit better.

I drove past the shop on my way home, saw Jacy Dean's hot pink van out front, knew she was there alone, and still didn't stop. Absence may make the heart grow fonder, but at times, it becomes the bricks we use to build walls around our hearts. This had to be one of those times because I wouldn't ask her to choose sides in the split between Neena and me. The pain made me want to go home, curl into a ball, and not come out again for a month.

But if I went back into hermit mode, Patrea would follow through on her offer to kick my sorry butt all over town, and I had no doubt she meant that literally, so I opted to go home and take my dog for a walk. Molly didn't care if I saw ghosts or if I chased murderers to help the not-quite-dearly-departed. Molly had come to me through one of those ghosts, and as much as I'd rather that hadn't been the how or why of it all, I was glad she was mine. Her unconditional love provided me with a great deal of solace.

Inside, I stashed the oranges in the fridge, and changed into warmer clothes. With Thanksgiving just around the corner, the air already felt like winter, but we hadn't yet had our first snow of the season. Ever hopeful, Molly watched me, and when I went for the hook where we kept her leash, she launched into her happy-dog dance.

Before clipping on the lead, I bent to hug

her. "Come on, pretty girl. Let's go."

Since my job requires me to be on call, I tucked my phone in my pocket along with my debit card and some spare cash, but wasn't expecting it to ring. Most days, I felt guilty taking a salary for a job that hardly ever required any work. But then, a tenant would move out and leave me a mess to clean, or I'd find myself belly-down in a crawlspace, dodging cobwebs while trying to thaw water pipes, and the guilt went away.

We hit the porch steps just as Neena pulled up in front of her garage. Losing a friend is bad enough. Losing a friend who lives across the street is just plain awkward. My first instinct was to turn around and go right back inside, but I stomped it down, tilted my chin up, and followed Molly down the stairs. No more hiding, no more skulking to avoid Neena, either. That was my new plan, and I was sticking to it.

She saw me. I saw her. We both turned away. I closed off my heart to ignore the sorrow that briefly washed over Neena's face. If she felt bad for cutting me out of her life, that was fine by me. I let Molly take the lead.

A sleek and shining bullet the color of good chocolate, the dog headed toward what qualified as the business district of Mooselick River. Ruled by her stomach, Molly most likely hoped to fetch up at the back door of the Blue Moon Diner, where the owner, Mabel, might give her a snack. Mabel had a fondness for dogs so long as they belonged to others, and Molly knew a soft touch when she met one.

I hadn't been to the diner since Patrea dragged me out of the house after the ugly Jober Peavey debacle. Since Mabel also had a fondness for me, I figured she'd forgive me for temporarily deserting her. I might have to eat crow first, but as long as Mabel cooked it, the crow would taste delicious.

Except it was Thea Lombardi who came out the back door of the diner to toss a bag in the trash.

"Hey, Thea. How's things?" Not my favorite person most of the time, Thea had helped catch Jober's killer even if it cost her a potential roll in the hay. I figured we'd saved her from hopping into bed with a murderer, so she should be grateful.

"Same as always." Thea looked me up and down, her expression critical. She didn't do grateful. "You look like crap. Cute dog, though." She bent to let Molly give her a sniff. Surprisingly, Molly leaned in when Thea scratched her behind the ears. There must be more to Thea than her off-putting exterior because my dog is an excellent judge of character.

"Thanks. I guess," I said. "What's on special today?"

"Never mind the special. I'll fix you something better." Mabel stood behind the screen door since Thea had left the metal security door open when she came out. "Thea, go check if table three needs a coffee refill."

Shrugging, Thea accepted the dismissal and passed her boss as Mabel stepped outside for a chat. To my utter shock, the diner owner pulled me in for a rough hug.

"What was that for?" I wrinkled my forehead.

Mabel held me at arm's length. "Have you been living under a rock?"

"Not literally. I've been helping Patrea with her latest project. Why? Did I miss something?" Quite likely, given how little contact I'd had with the outside world lately.

"I figure you were the one who convinced that tour bus company to add a stop in Mooselick River on their way to Hackinaw."

I shrugged. "I may have made a call or two, but we didn't cement any sort of deal."

"Whatever you said must have worked. We've had tour buses coming through three days a week!" More excited than I'd ever seen her, Mabel clapped her hands. "If this keeps up, I'll need to hire more help on bus days. Didn't Jacy mention they've been mobbed? The new craft store is booming.

Leandra's making a killing with her books and potions, and there's talk of a few more shops opening up. Martha Tipton has been going around taking credit for bringing Mooselick River back from the dead, but I figure it was your doing and not hers."

"I wondered why she hadn't been hounding me about this year's festival of lights. Well, she's welcome to take the credit if it gets me off that particular hook." Figuring Mabel didn't need to hear about my personal business, I glossed over the Jacy comment. "It was just a couple of phone calls. Not that big of a deal."

"It was more than that." Mabel put on her stubborn face—the one that used to scare the pants off her roller derby opponents. "When that bus broke down here, you could have arranged for the school bus to take those tourists to Hackinaw, but instead, you saw an opportunity that most of us would have missed. You got them to stay in Mooselick River, and more, you got them to explore what we have to offer. You rallied us all into taking care of them, and then you went above and beyond to put our town on the company's radar. I don't call that a small deal."

I couldn't help myself. She made me smile. "Okay, maybe I did do all of that." Her appreciation spread like a balm over some of the hurt places in my soul. "You're welcome."

"Give me fifteen minutes, and I'll fix you up a lunch that will make you want to slap your mother."

And there was a mental image I couldn't see ever coming to life.

"Will do." I led Molly away. Might as well spend that time getting her ya yas out.

CHAPTER THREE

I'd just driven down this same street on the way home from the grocery store, but being preoccupied with my personal life, I hadn't noticed the small changes I now saw as Molly and I made our way through the heart of town. Another formerly-abandoned building had brown paper taped on the inside of windows that had been dark for several years. Inside, saws buzzed, and hammers pounded out the sounds of progress.

Not only were the bait shop windows

cleaner than I'd ever seen them, but there had also been an attempt at creating an artistic display in the larger of the two. A scarecrow, most likely left over from the half-hearted Halloween decorating attempt, had traded in a straw hat for one with fishing hooks in the brim, sat in a camp chair, a bait bucket by his side, and a fishing pole in gloved hands.

My heart swelled with pride as we turned to walk back the way we had come. Molly tried to pull me across the street like everything was normal, but I didn't want to pass directly in front of Curated Collections, Jacy and Neena's shop.

I know I said no more skulking. I might have lied. And it wasn't exactly skulking to walk down the opposite sidewalk with my dog, anyway. In my heart, I knew Jacy wouldn't abandon me, but my head wasn't listening to my heart. Maybe if she didn't have to deal with me for a while, she wouldn't be dragged in two different directions. I owed her that much.

Say whatever you want, it sounded like logic in my head, and besides, my fifteen minutes were almost up, and I needed to get back to the diner. For that reason, I opted to take the shortcut accessed by dodging down the narrow space beside Drew's fitness center and cutting along the back of his block and across an empty lot to come out near the rear of the diner.

Sensing she was in for a treat, Molly loped along, pulling me into a jog as the diner came in sight. When Delilah Cannon stepped into our path, we nearly ran her down.

"Whoa, Molls." I gripped her leash as Molly skidded to a stop and gave the new person a gentle sniff.

"Does your dog bite?" Delilah froze in place as a low growl vibrated Molly's throat.

"No. Her name is Molly, and she's usually quite friendly." Since we were near enough, when Mabel stepped out to check if we were there, Molly proved the point by dancing up to her and wiggling all over. It probably had something to do with the hunk of chicken wrapped in bacon that Mabel offered, but there was no denying the change in the dog's demeanor.

Mabel gave Delilah a guarded look, attempted to wave away the cash I pulled out of my pocket, then frowned when I stepped forward and tucked the twenty into her apron pocket.

"Thanks for the food. It smells incredible. I can't wait to go home and dig in." That last was for Delilah's benefit, and to punctuate that fact, I gave Mabel a tiny wink. Mabel might move slowly, but she's a quick thinker and caught on.

"You run right along, now. I didn't go to all this trouble just for you to let my good cooking get cold." Mabel winked back. You have to love it when someone gets you.

I turned back to Delilah. "Hey, sorry to run off, but you heard the woman."

Without feeling so much as a shred of remorse, I left Delilah blinking at me and jogged away with Molly happily taking the lead. I congratulated myself on getting out of a conversation I'd rather not have.

The bullet-dodging lasted only as long as it took Delilah to get back to her car and catch up to me on my way home. We made quite the spectacle with her driving along at a snail's pace behind me, honking her horn and trying to get me to accept a ride. People looked out their windows, and I'm sure at least five different versions of the story had circulated through town before I got home.

When I did, I followed Molly inside and closed the door hoping Delilah would take the hint but knowing she wouldn't. She proved me right in less than a minute. When the doorbell rang. I sighed and accepted the inevitable but blocked the door to keep her from walking in.

"What can I do for you, Delilah? As you know, I've just picked up my lunch and planned to eat it before it got cold."

Seriously, that hint flew so low it nearly parted her hair, but it still went over her head.

"Didn't you see me following you? I would have given you a ride, and then you wouldn't have had to worry about cold food."

I'm sure my innocent expression fooled no one, but I put it on anyway. "I'm sorry, but Molly needed the exercise. Maybe another time." I stepped back to close the door, but she nudged her way in, a takeout bag from Mabel's in her hand and a smile beaming across her face.

"I've brought my lunch, so we can eat together and then get down to business."

"I wasn't aware we had any business," I said as I shrugged off my coat and led her to the kitchen. I wasn't kidding about eating my lunch and if I had to put up with Delilah while I did, whatever Mabel had made for me smelled worth it. "Other than me trying to find you a place to stay, which wasn't going to happen on just two days' notice. Where are you staying, anyway?"

Delilah shed her coat and followed me, making herself comfortable at the table while I pulled a pitcher of iced tea from the fridge. She sipped on the straw of her to-go cup while I poured myself a glass.

"I'm staying at the Marlow for the time being, but I'm not here to talk about that right now. I'm here to talk about Davina," she said. "I did tell you why I wanted to come."

"You did, but I'm not sure what your book has to do with me." I couldn't wait anymore. Mabel's slap-your-mother meal consisted of a hunk of hot sausage fried to perfection, cut in half, and smothered with onions and peppers on a homemade sub roll with a side of sweet potato fries. "I only ever met Davina the one time before she was…before she passed."

I told the truth, and even if it wasn't the entire truth, it wasn't a lie, so I didn't even feel bad for the attempt at deception. Delilah had no idea the line she was asking me to walk, and I wasn't about to draw her a diagram.

"You'd be better off talking to Leandra Wade. She knew Davina better than anyone besides her family." Or maybe even including them.

I'd been trying to pry details out of the dead woman ever since her afterlife had become my current-life problem. Davina wasn't the most forthcoming of ghosts. Despite being strangled to death with a beaded necklace, she swore she had no enemies, which was just plain silly, and I'd had to resort to drastic measures in my search for a possible motive.

All these weeks later, I was no closer to knowing where to look for her killer than I'd been on the day I found her body. As Davina's biggest self-professed fan, Delilah still occupied a spot on my list of potential murderers. I'd mostly decided she wasn't the one, and she was now at the very bottom of the list, but until I had definitive proof, she stayed.

Delilah leaned forward and pitched her voice low. "You wanna hear a secret?"

No.

"I guess," I said because she seemed unlikely to take no for an answer.

"There is no book. I figured if I said I was writing one, her friends and family would be more willing to talk to me. You have no idea the lengths people will go to for their fifteen minutes of fame."

Like turning yourself into a carbon copy of your idol and letting someone hire you to pretend to be her ghost? It took an effort, but I kept that thought to myself.

"I've come," Delilah added, "to solve her murder, and I need your help."

"Why me?"

I didn't realize I'd spoken out loud until Delilah responded.

"Why not you? I only met you the one time, but that was enough to get a sense of your character. You'll help me." Delilah picked up her take-out cup, sipped, then gestured with it. "You won't be able to help yourself. I know a do-gooder when I meet one, and that's you right down to the ground. You know this town and all of the players, so you'll have the inside perspective I'll need, and you don't seem to quibble at getting your hands dirty."

Words failed me for a moment, then I said, "I think that's the least flattering thing anyone has ever said to me."

"Wasn't meant to be." Delilah popped the plastic top on the salad she'd ordered, took out the little container of dressing, and set it aside. "Do-gooders make the world go around." She speared a forkful of greens. "I looked you up, you know."

"Shouldn't have taken long to do given the amount of news coverage around my divorce."

"Did you really find your ex in a hotel room?" It was the question everyone asked, so I was used to it by now.

I nodded and anticipated the second half of the question. "Naked and chained to the bed." Because he'd been such a jerk, the memory always made me smile. It probably always would.

"I think that might make you my hero," Delilah smiled. "You'll help me, won't you?"

"Yes." I agreed, but only because she might have or be able to find the information I needed and if by some slim chance I'd misjudged her and she was the killer—because it's a well-documented TV crime fact that murderers sometimes insert themselves into an investigation—keeping her close was a good idea. "I suppose I will."

Satisfied, Delilah got down to business. "I think our first suspect has to be Leandra Wade. She stood to gain the most from Davina's death."

Before she finished, I was already shaking my head.

"Absolutely not. For one, Leandra had no idea she was named in the will before Davina's untimely death. For another, I've known the woman since I was five years old, and I can tell you she's the last person in the world who would commit murder for financial gain. And if you need one more reason, she considered turning down the bequest entirely."

Because she got into a tiff with ghostly Davina, but Delilah didn't need to know that part. Telling people about ghosts had gone off my to-do list when Neena dumped me as a friend. Anyone who mattered to me already knew. Everyone else could suck it.

"So she says." Delilah gave what I assumed was meant to be a sage nod. "But people don't always tell the truth."

"Leandra does. If you don't piss her off, she'll be a great source of information. Besides, she has an alibi, so you can just trust me and take her off your suspect list."

"Fine," Delilah said. "But I'll point out that she *did* accept the bequest and *is* making a living off Davina's assets, but whatever you say. She's off the list. Anyone else I need to knock off the list for no good reason other than your blind faith?"

I leaned back in my chair, crossed my arms over my chest, and gave Delilah a taste of her own medicine.

"No, but if we're going to go there, why don't you tell me your whereabouts at the time of the murder? If we're talking motive, we should consider the statistics about how often stalkers turn into killers when the object of their interest doesn't return their affection."

Despite certain evidence to the contrary, I'm not stupid enough to poke a bear, but I have accidentally flicked water on a kitten before, and it puffed up about the same way Delilah did. She spit fury and indignation.

"Stalker? I was not a stalker. Davina and I had a relationship. Do you seriously think I would kill my best friend?"

"Not really, but I don't think Leandra would kill one of hers, either. You have more in common with her than you think."

Now, Delilah sniffed. "Davina didn't leave me a business with thousands and thousands of dollars worth of stock, so I guess that's where you're wrong."

"Well, I guess that says more about your friendship than it does about Leandra," I snapped. "Look, I appreciate that you're trying to come at things with an open mind, and I know, probably better than you do, that anyone will kill if they're pushed hard enough, but it was not Leandra."

"Who, then?"

I shrugged. "I wish I knew. Davina moved back here to spend time with her family and childhood friends. She opened a shop that created controversy among certain factions, but Ernie ruled out everyone involved in the protest, which was peaceful enough as these things go. Not exactly the type of heated situation that leads to a motive for murder."

"She wasn't murdered until she moved here, so I think location answers the motive question, don't you?"

If she talked to me like I was a child one

more time, I might just let Davina have a ghostly go at Delilah. She was the most tedious woman I'd had to deal with in quite some time.

"I can't help but think it had to be someone connected to one of her cases. This is a small town where people notice strangers, but no one has come forward to say they saw anyone out of place."

Delilah cocked an eyebrow and twisted her lips into a smirk. "Oh, I wouldn't count on the locals for being eagle-eyed. After all, no one noticed me until you caught me on Halloween morning, which is another reason I came to you specifically. You're observant."

"That's where you're wrong." I waggled a finger at her. "I knew you were in town before the Halloween event. In fact, I heard you knocking things over in the town office bathroom when I was there the day before. You should also know I went there looking for you because Robin Thackery told me she'd seen Davina skulking around town. Alive and well. Even if she got the circumstances wrong, she had you nailed, and she wasn't the only one who saw you. Several people did, so you're not as sneaky as you think you are."

Triumph turned to chagrin. "I didn't know that," Delilah admitted.

"Now, you do." Sighing, I ended the game of tit for tat, but I'd seen a way to keep her busy and out of my hair. At least for a while. "I have a list of people connected to Davina that live here in town, but since you attended so many tapings, maybe you'd know if there was anyone who didn't make it onto the show and carried a grudge. Or even someone who did and didn't get what they wanted. If we had more information on the people involved in her readings, we might find someone with a strong motive."

"Fine. If you want to chase your tail, go ahead. I'll be looking for the murderer right here where it happened."

Annoyed, Delilah rose to leave. I didn't try to stop her.

CHAPTER FOUR

When my phone rang during breakfast the next morning, and I saw Martha Tipton's name on the caller ID, I suppressed the urge to throw my phone in the dishwasher and run it through the pots and pans cycle.

"Hi, Martha. What can I do for you today?" I asked the question I didn't want answered.

"We have to do something about that new craft shop in town."

Pain settled between my eyes. "What's wrong with the craft shop?" I hadn't been in to check out the newest addition to the business section of downtown Mooselick River because I'd been too busy licking my wounds of late.

Martha harrumphed. "They're selling…I can't even form the words to describe something so scandalous. You'll have to go down there and see for yourself. I'll be expecting your call once you have. Then we'll decide what to do about the situation." She rang off without a goodbye.

Frowning, I set my phone aside and returned to eating my cereal before it got too soggy.

"I take it there's a scandal," Drew said. "Martha's voice tends to carry."

"So she says. You want to go with me? See what the fuss is all about?"

Eyes alight with humor, Drew shook his head. "Crafts scandal? No, I think I'll pass.

Why don't you call Jacy? Sounds like something she would appreciate."

I knew he was only trying to help, but I shut him down. "I'll get Patrea to go with me. I was planning to visit the flip house today anyway. I want to check how things are going. Maybe help out a little unless I get a work call."

Drew shrugged. "Whatever you think is best."

To keep him from elaborating, I picked up my phone and sent Patrea a text. Two seconds passed before she responded with a thumbs-up emoji. "There, it's all set."

Even though I sensed he had more he'd like to say, he let the subject of Jacy drop. At least until he kissed me goodbye on his way out the door for work. "You know how when we're watching movies and the whole conflict could be resolved if one main character just talked to the other?"

So what if his comment made sense? Didn't he realize that if I never put Jacy on the spot, she wouldn't have to choose between her oldest and newest friends? My system was working, and I planned on sticking to it.

"Leave me to my avoidance of the issue, please."

After he'd gone, I hugged Molly goodbye and left to meet Patrea at Knit Up. She pulled into the space behind me about a minute after I arrived. "What's the deal?" She wanted to know. "You mentioned Martha and a scandal. I'm dying of curiosity."

"Same. You know everything I know at the moment. Shall we go inside and see what she's talking about?"

"Wild horses couldn't stop me now. I do love a good scandal."

"Don't get your hopes up too high," I said. "Martha practically exists to make a big deal out of nothing. I mean, they're selling yarn and knitted stuff. How bad could it be?"

At first, it wasn't bad at all. The store was laid out nicely, with racks and bins of yarn and crochet cotton in every shade and color of the rainbow. Cheerful colors in lots of textures. Soothing. Because it practically called out to me, I ran a finger across a skein of pink chenille so soft it tempted me to buy a pair of needles. What I might do with them defied rationality.

"Kind of makes you want to take up knitting, doesn't it?" Pointing to a prominent sign, Patrea echoed my thoughts. "They offer classes. What do you say we sign up?"

Was it genuine interest? Or simply Patrea's way of getting me out of the house?

"I'll think about it. Not seeing the scandal here. You?" I moved deeper into the store and found a selection of charming, handmade items.

Patrea followed. "Not so far. But I think I need that matching hat and mittens." She picked up a plastic shopping basket from a nearby rack, tossing in three sets of hats and mittens in different shades. When I cocked an eyebrow at her, she simply said, "Christmas."

Lulled into thinking Martha had lost her grasp on reality, we browsed our way toward the back of the store, where the shopkeepers had set up a display of handcrafted items for the kitchen. Patrea lagged behind me just a few steps to run her hand over a chunky blanket wrought from fluffy, white yarn, so I got the first glimpse of what we'd come there to find and froze while my brain tried to process what I was seeing.

For once, Martha had seen scandal where it actually existed, and before I could stop myself, I snorted out a laugh.

"What?" Patrea stepped up beside me, followed my gaze to where it was riveted, and then, she saw for herself. "What are those supposed to be?"

"I'd guess they're pot handle cozies or something. I don't know the technical term."

"They look like—" words failed Patrea.

"They do." Biting my lip didn't stop the laughter as I stared at the display of crocheted tubes with rounded tips that wouldn't have looked out of place if there'd been a rack of whips and pasties nearby. "Do you think it's on purpose?"

"Has to be." Patrea's eyes danced. "Unless those ridges near the tip serve some actual function."

I'd begun to wheeze by then. "Like for getting a better grip, you mean?"

Patrea hooted and waggled her eyebrows. "It's always important to get a good grip."

"Dirty!" I pointed at her and laughed harder. When confronted with what looked like a rainbow display of male genitalia, anything you say will sound dirty. Just trust me on that one.

Drawn by the sounds of mirth, the woman running the store walked over to ask if we needed help.

"I'm pretty sure there's nothing anyone can do to help us now," Patrea said, then tried to get hold of herself when the shopkeeper frowned.

"These pan-handle cozies are some of our best sellers. People can't seem to pass them up. Especially the tourists. They love them so much they even pose in front of the display." Either she didn't see it or consciously decided to ignore the obvious. "I bet they're going to be poking out of a lot of Christmas stockings this year."

I just about choked as I tried to hold back a belly laugh over that visual.

"I think we'd better check out now." Patrea practically dragged me to the register and managed to keep herself under control enough to pay for her purchases.

Back on the street, we laughed until we

cried and could barely stand.

"That is the best thing I've seen all week," Patrea said. "What are you planning to tell Martha?"

"Don't say her name to me while I can still see them in my head. It hurts my brain."

It took a few minutes to settle, during which time I spied Delilah Cannon walking along the main street, her face a set mask, and heading for Leandra's shop. Thus ended my fit of giggles.

"Damn it." I grabbed Patrea's arm and dragged her along behind me. "She's going there. I just know it."

"Who? Where and why?"

"Delilah. She's determined Leandra had something to do with Davina's death."

Patrea stopped dead. "That's ridiculous."

"Beyond the telling," I agreed, then ducked

down the narrow alley between two buildings to get to the back entrance of the shop, which should have been locked, but wasn't because Leandra wouldn't see the need to bother. "We'll just sneak in here and listen."

I didn't want to see Leandra if I could help it, but I wouldn't hesitate to step in if Delilah got nasty. We got into place just as Delilah introduced herself.

"I'm writing a book about Davina Benet, and since you were one of her closest friends, I hoped you wouldn't mind answering a few questions."

"I'd be delighted," Leandra said, cheerful as ever. "Davina was a dear person to me. Oh, the stories I could tell."

"You'd have to say that, wouldn't you? Given the spoils of her death."

"Spoils," Leandra might come off as fluffy-headed and vague. She was anything but. "You mean the shop?"

"It's a nice shop." The implication speared sharply through Delilah's attempt at a mild tone. "A step up for you, no?"

"What's going on?" Davina popped up just in time to hear Leandra's response.

"Are you implying I'd murder my oldest friend for her business? What kind of book are you writing?"

"Delilah," Davina all but growled.

"Davina's here," I told Patrea so it wouldn't look like I was talking to myself when I cautioned, "Let it play out, okay? Leandra can hold her own; if Delilah goes too far, I'll handle it. You don't need to—" I didn't get to finish because she was gone. "And now she's not."

Patrea's eyes went wide, but that was the only indication that things were taking a turn for the weird.

"She bothering you?" I heard Davina speak to Leandra. Great.

"Leandra can see her?" Patrea's eyes widened.

"Well, yeah. It's a thing. I'll explain later."

"I'm not implying anything," came the answer to Leandra's earlier question. "But I've read the police reports. You went home to "get something" and didn't return until Davina was dead, which means your husband is the only one who can verify your alibi." Delilah picked up on the only point that seemed to matter to her. "No one else saw you from the time you say you left the shop until you returned after the body had been found."

"Unless you count the mailman, Viola Montayne, and Bess Tate."

Silence is the sound of someone climbing down off their high horse.

"Excuse me?"

"The mailman delivered just as I was leaving my house. We waved at each other, as you do when you're the neighborly sort. When I pulled back into town, I saw Bess's car on the side of the road, so I stopped to see if she needed help, but she was just talking to her nephew on her cell phone."

"I see," Delilah sounded very much as if she wished she didn't.

"And Viola Montayne cut me off as I turned onto the main road. I may have given her the finger, and she may have returned the favor."

"Good one, Lee," Davina said.

"So you see, I couldn't have killed Davina."

Shut down, Delilah dithered for a moment but couldn't formulate another accusation. When Leandra offered Delilah a free nerve tonic sample, Davina snorted. "Hope you have a gallon of it."

But the tension had gone. Delilah made apologetic noises, and Leandra remained gracious as always.

"I think we're fine here," I said to Patrea and headed back outside. "Crisis averted."

I followed Patrea back to the flip house, where a crew of men busily nailed new shingles on the roof ahead of oncoming winter. We picked our way past the construction dumpster full of old shingles and onto the porch filled with narrow boxes.

"The windows came this morning. They'll get started on those as soon as the roof is finished, which should be tomorrow if there are no surprises. It's too late in the season for exterior paint, but we're shooting to have the bulk of the structural work done and the place buttoned up before the first major snowstorm hits."

"It's coming along faster than I expected. You don't waste time when you put your mind to something, do you?"

Patrea shrugged, but I sensed the compliment pleased her. "I expect I'll still be stripping wallpaper when the Easter bunny hops into town, but I'm having a blast." She took me around to see her progress since I'd been there last and then handed me a pair of rubber gloves.

"Are we cleaning toilets or something?"

"Not today." Waving for me to follow, Patrea headed down the hallway to the small room she was using to store supplies. "Grab some of that steel wool and a couple of rags."

While I did as she asked, Patrea poured denatured alcohol into a pair of containers. "Today, we're going to do magic."

The sharp scent of the alcohol tickled my nose in a way that suggested her definition of magic and mine were not the same, but I followed her back to the front hall, where she set the containers on a small table covered with plastic and newspaper.

"See how the finish on the banister and rails looks cracked and crazed? That's layer upon layer of old polish, and as it ages and dries, it creates this desert sand sort of texture."

Nodding, I ran my hand over the wood, which didn't look that much different from the banisters at my house. "How do you fix it?" I'd assumed the process involved harsh chemical strippers or, worse, professional intervention.

"Watch this." Taking the steel wool from me, Patrea broke off a hunk, dipped it into the alcohol, and began gently scrubbing the side of the banister. She dipped the dirty steel back into the alcohol every so often, turning it mucky. The section of wood lost that dark, cracked look as the finish smoothed out and lightened considerably.

"The alcohol removes layers of dirt while it dissolves the old finish. See how much better it looks already? We don't want to remove the patina entirely. We only want to redistribute the old varnish, which keeps the wood protected. Magic, right?"

I had to agree on one level, and then she

hit me with the zinger.

"Your banisters could use a touch of magic, don't you think? The stairs, too."

"Only if I had a place to move into for a week. That stuff stinks, and I'm getting lightheaded."

"Meh. Do yours in the summertime, keep the windows open and put some fans in them. You'll hardly smell a thing, and you'll thank me when it's done."

"Doubtful."

But I probably would. The banister was beginning to look fantastic. Drat her. Now, I wanted mine to look the same. House envy. Apparently, it's a thing.

"I'm thinking." Moving around me, Patrea began on the section above where I worked. "You said you don't see ghosts everywhere, but this house is old enough to have at least one, right?" She seemed jazzed at the possibility.

"Maybe." I shrugged. "Mine doesn't, or so I've been told by one of the ghosts."

The soft sound of steel wool rubbing against old wood went on for a minute before she responded.

"Ghosts can see other ghosts? I'm still hazy on the who-what-and-how of this whole veil thing."

"Join the club. I'm the president. You can be the treasurer. We'll meet weekly to shake our heads and eat cookies. As treasurer, you're in charge of the cookies."

"You only invited me because my cookies are the best."

I had to laugh. "That's a given, but you do have other qualities. Anyhow, I can ask Davina to check this place out the next chance I get."

"It might be a selling point for the right buyer."

"You won't need a resident ghost to sell this place. Not the way it's coming together. Have you decided on a real estate agent?"

Patrea grinned. "I have, but I was thinking I could have you get Martha Tipton on board. She'd sell it faster, and I wouldn't have to give up a percentage of the take."

"The woman could sell widgets to a widget maker, so you're probably not wrong there."

We finished the banister just as Delilah texted me to request my presence at the inn for a conversation about her recent findings.

CHAPTER FIVE

The steps of the Marlow Inn seemed to stretch on forever and looked steep enough to make my calves weep at the sight of them. That was my fear turning up the heat on my imagination. I hadn't returned to the inn since the Ghostly Caper From Hell That Ruined My Life. And yes, that is the official title of The Night Everything Changed. In my head, anyway.

I didn't appreciate Delilah dragging me over here, but the alternative was my place, and I didn't want her to think it was okay to hang out there at every given opportunity. She hadn't gone for my suggestion of meeting at the Blue Moon since it wasn't the most private place to chat about sensitive subjects.

"Suck it up, Dupree," I told myself out loud. What was the worst that could happen? Other than another friend treating me the same way as Neena. Except, David Barrington had become family to me, and not just because my parents had taken him in at a time when he needed a safe place to heal, either. After a rocky start—my fault— we'd formed close ties. Nerves stretched their spiny roots down into my gut. I could feel them twining around like snakes.

The steps took on their normal size when I put my foot on the bottom one and banished all negative thoughts as I did. Or as many as I could manage, anyway. But it still sounded like the doors of doom echoing shut behind me when I stepped inside. Everything looked the same as the last time I was there, but I felt different. Exposed. Vulnerable.

At the front counter, David looked up. Gave me his usual grin. "It lives."

I shrugged off about a thousand pounds of the weight I'd been carrying.

"Was there any doubt?"

Shrugging, David said, "Not especially. It just feels like it's been a while. You have great timing since I brought something back from my trip to Vermont." He drew a container of maple syrup from under the counter and set it on top. "For you, from my folks. It's grade B, which I like better than grade A. It's darker, more density of flavor, and not quite as sweet."

I frowned as I joined him behind the desk and took the plastic jug from him. "I didn't know you were planning a visit home. When did you leave? How long were you gone?"

He shrugged again. "I wasn't. They had an early storm with freezing rain. My dad slipped on the ice and broke his leg badly enough to need emergency surgery. Since we're in the lull between leaf peeping and the holidays, I left Nanette in charge and spent a couple of weeks helping out while he got through the initial recovery phase. I only got back last night. Late."

And here, I'd accused him of cutting me off when he was in the middle of a family drama. Lesson one? The world does not revolve around Everly Dupree.

"He's okay? The surgery went well?"

David nodded. "He's got some rehab ahead of him, but the docs put him back together well enough, and he was hitting the crabby phase of convalescence when I escaped…I mean, left. The plus side is that Nanette held down the fort like a champ."

"You could have called me. I'd have been happy to help out."

Leaning sideways, David offered me a rare, one-armed hug. "I know that, and if I'd stayed another week, I probably would have made that call since we have some folks booked in for the weekend of Thanksgiving. But between you and me, I wanted to test Nanette's management skills. I'm thinking of giving her a raise and more responsibility. I can always hire someone to clean part-time, but running an inn was never in my life plan. If she's willing to take it on, I think I might look into what it would take to renew my EMT certification. Maybe split my time between here and working shifts."

Because this was a huge step forward for him, and I knew he wouldn't appreciate it if he saw me get all misty-eyed, I clamped down on my emotions.

"The ambulance service could use someone like you. You'd make a fantastic addition to the team."

I said nice things, so why did he look pained? The answer came when he changed the subject and finally addressed the elephant in the room.

"So, that night at the bar."

"What about it?" I cocked an eyebrow and, remembering my vow to hang my head no more, stared him down.

"You okay?"

"I guess," I said. "Depends on how you define, okay. No lasting physical damage, anyway."

"You could have told me." There was no censure in his tone. "But I can see why you didn't. I've kept my share things private, so trust me, I get it." He patted my hand, which also wasn't a characteristic gesture for him. We were two for two today.

"Thanks." I put my hand over his. "I wanted to tell you. More than once, actually, but you never know how people will respond when they hear something weird, and when I moved back home, my life took a turn in that direction."

"It happens."

"So it does." Delilah appeared at the top of the staircase, saw me, and waved. "Speaking of weird. I have to go. We'll talk more later, okay?"

"Game night this week?" If he didn't know we weren't doing them anymore, he hadn't been talking with Neena while he was gone. I shook my head.

"Not this week." There wasn't time for an explanation because I had to deal with Delilah, and even if there had been, I didn't feel like rehashing a painful topic. "Not with it being Thanksgiving, anyway. After that, I'm not sure. We'll have to see."

I left him sitting there and wondered if things would ever be the same again. It certainly didn't feel like it to me.

Delilah willingly followed me into what I considered a safe space, the inn's dining room. "This is a nice place, but at the rate things are going, I expect I'll be in town longer than I planned, so I will need to find a place that's a little less expensive. Did you have any luck finding me a short-term, furnished rental?"

"Not exactly. We're a small town with fewer amenities than you're probably used to. Not a lot of call for furnished rooms to let. Or for AirBnB type accommodations." Yet, anyway. But if things kept going as they were, we might see some changes.

"I have four weeks of paid vacation time accrued and two weeks of sick leave that I'm planning to use if it takes longer than that. And I have a little nest egg that will buy a little more time if necessary," Delilah confided. "but my finances don't run to an extended stay in a place as nice as this. I'd be willing to consider renting just a room in someone's house if anyone has one going begging."

The veil Delilah tossed over that hint was of the moth-eaten lace variety. She pushed the issue when I didn't immediately offer her a room at my house. "There has to be something. You're holding out on me."

A solution occurred, and since it didn't involve her moving in with me, the angels sang.

"There's the Bide-A-Way. I know the owner pretty well, and she owes me a favor for cleaning up after the guests from hell. I guess I could call and see if I can get you the friends and family discount."

"That would be perfect," Delilah said, and then, when I didn't immediately pull out my phone, gave me a pointed stare.

"I'll just do that right now."

"Fantastic," Delilah beamed. "I'll see if Jason has something to nibble on while we work. He's an artist in the kitchen."

Since Barb had just picked up the phone, I waved Delilah away and called in the favor. I'd barely hung up before Delilah returned with a plate of cheese, fruit, and crackers.

"It's all set," I told her the amount Barb had quoted me for a week's stay and gave her directions to the motel on the outskirts of town. "I gave Barb your name. She's expecting you. Just be there before she closes the office today, and you're all set."

"Good enough. Now, let's get down to business. I've got the police reports right here." A sheaf of papers landed on the table between us. "And it looks like your mother was a suspect for a while. I'll assume she's fully cleared." Delilah's voice went up at the end, making it more of a question than a statement.

"She was a suspect for a short time. But there's a big difference between waving a protest sign and committing murder. Ernie took her off the list quite quickly. And before you even ask, Patrea Evergreen was also cleared."

Selecting a crisp wafer I suspected Jason had baked from scratch, Delilah added cheese and salami. "Okay." She popped the cracker into her mouth and chewed while she looked at me speculatively. "Whatever you say."

"You're damned right I do. Look, I know you think you'll bring a fresh perspective to this investigation, and maybe you're right, but there's no need to rehash what's already been established."

"That's just it, though, isn't it? Very little has been established, which is why I've come. I intend to change all that."

Coupled with a supercilious head bob, her smarmy tone grated my last nerve down to the quivering end. If she thought I'd been dragging my feet to protect my mother, she would be more of a hindrance than a help. No surprise there.

"Okay," I challenged. "Why don't you tell me what you think was the motive? If you know so much about her, you must have some idea why someone wanted Lucy dead." I tossed in Davina's true name as a test.

"Lucy? Who's that?" She failed.

"Davina's birth name was Lucille Bennett." Don't know everything, do you?

Except she wanted me to think she did. "I forgot. That was before my time with her. But it shows I'm probably right about it being someone from around here. From what I've learned, your mother and Leandra Wade were Davina's closest childhood friends. Maybe you could tell me what their relationship was like."

Hadn't we had this conversation before? Nothing like going in circles the way Molly does when she chases her tail. For one reason or another, I'd been chasing mine since the moment I found Davina's body.

My eyes narrowed. "Not a factor."

"If you consider the timing, you must at least consider the possibility of a hometown feud. Resentment tends to fester over time, you know." Convinced she was right, Delilah continued. "So there's Davina, returning after her long sojourn away. Probably expecting a hero's welcome, and what does she get instead? She gets dead, that's what."

Wound up now, she would have kept going, I was sure, but I cut Delilah off before she named my mother as a suspect again. Too many instances of that, and I'd tell her where to stick her investigation and probably her head as well.

"Or, she found a missing person that needed to stay lost, and they or someone connected to them wasn't happy about it. The problem is that it could be a recent thing that she didn't tell anyone about. Or the killer waited until she'd retired and her guard was down to step in and take her out."

Weak motive, I knew, but I didn't have anything better because the timing made Delilah's theory the more sensible of the two, even if it felt all kinds of wrong to me.

Still, without more insight into Davina's final days, we might never find the trigger that set the killer off.

"Did she have security at her tapings?" I followed through on my theory and ignored Delilah's subtle eye roll.

"Of course. It's standard, I think."

"Is it, though?" Now I had her on the defensive. "My ex-father-in-law didn't hire security for his family until there'd been a credible threat. Seems like it would be the same with Davina's studio. Good security isn't cheap. What's it say in your police reports about that?"

We both reached for the sheets, but I beat her to them and scanned for information while she fumed. It didn't take long to find what I knew would be there because Davina had admitted as much to me already.

"See, there's a mention of threatening letters and emails." I flipped a page around so she could see for herself.

"Yes, but if you keep reading, you'll find none panned out."

"And if you'd get your mind off Mooselick River for just a minute, you'd realize that for every person who took the time to make their opinions heard, there are probably three more who let them fester in silence. The type of silence that eventually leads to retaliatory action. Now, weren't you supposed to make a list? Let's see it."

Delilah's face pinked. "I was busy and didn't get around to it."

Code for I didn't think it mattered, so I didn't bother.

"Okay," I said again, in a totally different tone. Jason had appeared in the doorway, caught my eye, and nodded toward the kitchen. I excused myself under the pretext of giving Delilah time to think. "Why don't you take a few minutes and do it now? I'll be right back."

I didn't expect her to make a list, but at least Jason had given me a break from her, and for that, I was grateful.

"What's up?" I snagged a cracker from the plate sitting on the counter, bit in, and sighed at the delicate crunch and flavor. "These are fantastic, by the way. What's in them?"

"Rosemary and a hint of lavender with pink sea salt."

"Well, it works."

The kitchen smelled of sugar and spice and all things nice as Jason cut maple leaves from a circle of pie crust, then carefully added veins and applied the results to the edges of a pumpkin pie nearly ready to go into the oven. I breathed in deeply and eyed the tray of tarts cooling on a rack with almost the same look I gave Drew when he strolled through the house wearing a towel.

"Thanks. I…uh…have a question."

"Hmm?" I'd been distracted by pastry.

"It's about your mom."

My mother? What was the deal today? Everyone wanted to talk about my mother. "What about her?"

He hemmed and hawed for a moment, then asked what felt like a random question. "Do you think she'd share her apple cider donut recipe from the Halloween event?"

My lips twitched. With more than a touch of gray at his temples, his face a little weathered, or maybe seasoned was the correct term, Jason was the kind of guy who looked like he'd been around the block a few times. He didn't talk about his past or his plans for the future outside of how he hoped to expand the offerings at the inn, so I found it amusing to picture him trading recipes with the good women of Mooselick River.

"I'm sure she would. She's not like my grandmother in that respect."

Jason shot me a quirked brow, so I explained, "Grammie Dupree, my dad's mother, was always happy to share a recipe—or a receipt as she called them—but she liked to alter the amounts on some of the ingredients a little. Just enough to make sure hers always tasted better. My mom doesn't do that."

"She seems like a nice person. Like one of the best." There was something in his voice that I could only identify as longing.

"She is the best." I might not have offered my opinion with the same conviction a year ago, but we'd worked through our differences—mainly by finding our similarities. "Do you want me to ask her for you? Or you could skip over to the library and talk to her. I'm sure she'd be flattered. They're excellent donuts."

"Maybe, I will." His attention seeming focused on the pastry forming under deft hands, Jason nodded. "Go ahead and take one of those tarts on your way out."

I'd been dismissed, but I didn't mind a bit since the tart softened the blow. "Thanks." I'm not ashamed that I dawdled and wolfed the tart down in three bites on my way back to the dining room.

"Took you long enough." When I returned to the table, Nanette was cleaning the delicate, frosted-glass sconces lining both sides of the room, and Delilah hadn't written down a single name.

I gestured to the blank page. "Doesn't look that way to me."

"I really don't see the point," Delilah raised her voice slightly. "In wasting my time making a list of Davina's old cases, so I'm not doing it. She helped people, and they loved her for it. The murder happened here, and it's here, among family and friends, that we'll find her killer. If you don't get that, you should go home and let me handle things from here on out."

"You know what? That's fine with me." Rising, I made my way over to Nanette. "Do you mind telling me what you're using on that glass? I have some lamps of similar vintage at home, and it's the devil's job to clean frosted glass. Is it another one of Leandra's cleaning formulas?"

Probably not because, for once, Nanette wasn't surrounded by the scent of essential oils.

Her face red, either with exertion or from eavesdropping, Nanette grinned and replied. "Hydrogen peroxide. That's it. Just spray it on, let it sit for a few seconds, and wipe. Works great on windows and mirrors, too. Fewer streaks."

"Thanks. I'll give it a shot." Without a backward glance at Delilah, I walked out the door and let my annoyed momentum carry me right out of the inn.

"Trouble in paradise?" Davina hovered

near my car.

"Shut up," I warned her. I was not in the mood, and a big part of that was her fault.

"You're both peeking under the wrong dust ruffles. I didn't have an enemy in the world."

"Keep believing that. See if it gets you any less dead, why don't you?"

I got in my car and spun up some loose gravel on my way out of the lot.

CHAPTER SIX

On the way home, I stopped by the library to ask my mother if she'd seen anyone strange hanging around Davina's shop the day she died. If Delilah wouldn't help and Davina wouldn't let go of her delusions, I'd have to find another source of information. Before I could do much more than offer a hello, she hit me with a question.

"I hate to ask at such short notice, but could you take Blue for a few days? I'd appreciate it if you could pick him up tomorrow and keep him through the weekend."

"This weekend? Are you going somewhere? It's Thanksgiving." We hadn't talked about it, but I'd assumed Drew and I would be spending the day with my folks since his parents were flying to the west coast to spend time with his sister and her family.

My mother's attention was more focused on checking in books than my shocked expression. She nodded. "We've been invited to Vermont for the holiday."

"Really? Wouldn't that be a bit inconvenient? I've just come from the inn, and David told me about Mr. Barrington's injury."

Mom stopped scanning barcodes for a moment. "That's exactly why we're going. When Wendy called last night, she sounded

108

frazzled. With everything they've been through these past couple of weeks, I thought it would be nice to go and help with the holiday cooking, so I shamelessly finagled an invite with that intention. You don't mind, do you?"

I did, but I wasn't about to say so.

"No, of course not. It's a lovely gesture, and I'm sure they'll appreciate you taking the time to pitch in." My mind had already begun forming a grocery list. "I hope they aren't out of turkeys at the grocery store. Otherwise, I'll be feeding Drew a Thanksgiving pot roast."

Eyes twinkling, Mom reached across the counter to pat my arm. "Oh, I don't think it will come to that. There's a twenty-three-pound bird thawing in my fridge that I have no intention of hauling on a road trip.

Consider it a consolation prize for taking the dog at a moment's notice."

"Twenty-three pounds? That's the size of a toddler. We'll be eating leftovers for a month."

"I did not need that mental image," My mother said. "David has no plans for the holiday, and I bet Neena's looking for an excuse to avoid eating with Viola. Two extra mouths should cut down on the leftovers."

I hadn't told her about Neena's and my drama or the rift, so I shrugged. "It's a bit late to invite people, but we'll see." It wasn't a lie so much as an omission of facts, but even so, I found it difficult to utter even the faintest of untruths while looking my mother in the eye, so I looked over her left shoulder.

"Something wrong, dear?"

Didn't work. I should have known.

Because tears threatened to sting, I shook my head and tried to brush her off. "I'm okay."

"Everly." How she could inject sympathy, concern, and a sense of mild frustration into a single word, I'll never know. Either way, the dam broke.

"Fine. I'm not okay. Neena hasn't spoken to me since the night Martin Warner went to jail." She got the abbreviated version of events, her eyes widening with every passing revelation. "I've been avoiding Jacy because if she's forced to choose a side, it might jeopardize her business."

By then, my voice had risen to a squeak. Mom produced a box of tissues from behind the counter, set them in front of me, then walked around to pull me in for a hug.

"I'm sorry. I know that doesn't seem like

much consolation right now."

I shrugged, dropped my head on her shoulder, and gave in to a serious case of the sobs. With my coloring, I'm not one of those pretty criers whose eyes glisten while a single tear slides down porcelain skin. Nope. Red hair and freckles over palest peach that goes red and blotchy if I even think about anything sad. That's me.

Flowers over citrus, her perfume took me back to when a hug solved all my problems.

"If I can catch Davina's killer and get her to cross over, and if she keeps her word about shutting the door behind her, maybe things can go back to normal."

I felt her body stiffen, and then she pulled back a little to look me in the eye.

"I'm all for whatever it is you think will make your life easier." Smiling in a not entirely comforting way, she tucked a curl behind my ear, then wiped away the last of my tears. "My experience with the paranormal hasn't been nearly as intense as yours, so I don't presume to understand. You've been thrust into a series of unfortunate circumstances."

The derisive snort popped out before I could stop it. "Right. Because I'm a tragedy magnet, and you're not."

She didn't argue the point exactly, but she did wrinkle her nose in distaste at the description.

"And you've done a great deal of good with your ability," Mom continued as if I hadn't spoken, and I noticed she chose the word ability over gift, which said a lot about her thoughts on the subject.

But not all.

"Good deeds are fine and wonderful if they don't land you in one dangerous situation after the other. For that reason, I support the closing of doors. But, and I can't believe I'm saying this, you can't let fear of what people think be the reason you walk away from what you're able to do."

Grabbing another tissue, I honked out enough snot to mostly clear my sinuses, but I still sounded like I'd been hit by the flu when I said, "I do enjoy helping people, but I miss my friends, and I feel like a failure for not making the best choices."

You always hear things about mother lions defending their cubs. I expect their eyes go all hard and glint dangerously like my mom's when they do. "Screw your friends."

My mouth dropped open since that was a phrase I never expected her to use. "Mom!"

Her hands went up to emphasize her point. "If they can't accept you for who you are, they don't deserve you, and they never did."

"Sorry to cry on your shoulder like that." But it felt good to have her support and even better to have had her comfort.

"That's what mothers are for. We can cancel the trip to Vermont if you need us to stay." The offer warmed my heart.

"No, you go. It will do dad good to see Mr. Barrington. I'll be fine. I'll miss you guys, though."

"You'll miss my famous Parker House rolls, you mean." A joke to relieve the tension.

A grin split my face. "Those, too. And your chocolate cream pie is sin on a stick."

"I'll email you the recipes for both."

Between the emotional conversation and the fact that my head had begun to fill with lists of things I'd need to buy to go with the turkey, I nearly forgot why I'd wanted to speak to her.

"Thanks." It all came back to me, but I waited until the library patron who had just come in brought her books to the counter to check them in. When she'd gone, and we were alone again, I asked, "I know we've talked about this before, but do you remember seeing anyone strange hanging around the day Davina was killed?"

"She still bugging you?"

"Less than you'd expect. Her friend Delilah is in town and has decided to turn her hand to a little crime-solving. With my help, of course."

Mom tilted her head when she appraised

me. "Does she know?"

I shuddered. "No, and I'm planning to keep it that way. She's a little," I struggled to find the right wording, "prone to fanaticism, I guess. I have better things to do than mediate a series of heart-to-heart conversations with her dead idol."

Nodding, my mom said, "I understand. Believe me." She went and got a pad of paper and a pen. "I can't say I saw anyone out of place that day, but there were so many people milling around. I'll make a list."

Organized to a fault, she broke the list into sections: one for the church group, one for the HAGS (Harmonic Association of Gifted Spiritualists), and one for everyone else. I didn't prod her while she worked it all out, closing her eyes several times to bring the memories into focus.

"I'm not sure how helpful this will be, but I think that's everyone." She spun the list and slid it across the counter so I could read the names. Not a single one stood out as a viable suspect. Still, I tore the sheet from the pad, folded it, and tucked it in my purse to peruse later. Maybe something would click.

"Thanks. If you think of anyone else, let me know. I've hit a wall with this one. It's everyone and no one as suspects. Davina's no help because she can't accept that someone disliked her enough to resort to murder."

"What about starting with the motive?"

Shrugging, I said, "What about it? The persons who most benefited from her death were Leandra and Tim's kids. Her family all have alibis, and even if they didn't, I don't get the vibe from any of them. We both know Leandra wouldn't commit murder. Not cold-blooded murder, and not for financial gain."

Nodding her agreement, mom said, "There are other things besides money that can drive people to kill." She'd probably read at least a thousand mystery books in her lifetime. "Love, revenge, to protect a secret, to protect family, moral or religious reasons, self-preservation." Her list was longer than mine had ever been. "And some kill out of sheer selfishness."

"That's all of them if you ask me. Unless we're talking self-defense." I brushed my hair back behind my ears. "The problem with applying all those theories to Davina is that I don't know enough about her to judge which ones might be possible. She spent most of her life elsewhere, so I'm floundering."

Mom pointed out the obvious. "Wouldn't her friend come in handy there?"

"You'd think." I huffed out a frustrated sigh. "But you'd be wrong. Delilah's convinced the culprit is someone from Davina's past. Someone who still lives in Mooselick River. She says the timing proves it had to be someone local, and I can't argue with her logic, but I want to. It just doesn't ring for me."

We cut short our murder discussion when Bess Tate walked through the library door.

"Hi, Bess. How have you been?" I hadn't seen Bess since Halloween.

"Just dandy. You talk to Martha lately? She's been keyed up for days over the latest scandal." The way Bess waggled her eyebrows, I knew exactly what she meant.

I nodded. "I have. And I've seen the offending items for myself."

"What offending items?" My mother wasn't up to speed.

"It seems one of the church ladies has been crocheting pot handle cozies that look a bit like," I paused to choose the right term.

"A man's wiener." Absolute glee lit Bess's expression. "In a rainbow of colors, no less."

My mother snorted.

"According to the clerk, those things are selling like hotcakes. Martha's worried the town will get a reputation for being the source of *crafts of a saucy nature*."

Bess giggled in a way that might be unnerving if you didn't know her. "I hope we do." Then she can let up with the never-ending list of ridiculous events. I had to talk her out of setting up a last-minute event for

Thanksgiving, but she's already making plans for Christmas.

Not a surprise to me or anyone who knew Martha. "The lighting contest was fun last year, and as much as I hate to admit it, these events have helped revitalize the town," I said in her defense.

"I'll remind you you said that when you're dragging her back from the deep end," Bess said, then turned to my mother. "You get that book I asked for?"

I took my cue to leave. "I'll pick Blue up tomorrow, have a great trip."

It looked like my mom might have wanted to say something more but couldn't. "I'll call you from the road."

CHAPTER SEVEN

Thanksgiving preparations had all but crowded ghosts and murders out of my thoughts the next morning as I added one or two more things to my grocery list.

"Four boxes of pre-made pie crusts?" Drew looked over my shoulder. "Are we having more people for dinner, then?"

"No," I said with maybe the slightest edge of hysteria creeping into my tone. "But you like apple pie, and my mom gave me her recipe for chocolate pie filling. Then there's pumpkin. It's not Thanksgiving without pumpkin pie."

"That's only three." He thought he was being helpful by pointing that out. He wasn't. "And those packaged deals come with double crusts, so two would be plenty."

"Unless I screw something up."

"Ah," he nodded as he refilled my coffee cup. "Your inner organizer kicked in, and you're planning for every contingency."

"It's the way I roll. You got a problem with that?"

"None at all."

Except he didn't sound sure.

"What? I'm sensing you have a problem."

I don't know what emotions registered on my face, but his went wide-eyed and guileless in the face of them. "No, I don't have a problem." He held his hands up as if to ward off an attack or something.

"Oh, I think you do." Was this our first fight?

Nope. You can't fight with Drew.

"I don't." Leaning down, he got on my eye level as I sat at the kitchen table in what I couldn't admit to myself was a stew of emotions that had nothing to do with pie. "You're spinning because Thanksgiving is a time for family, and you're already missing yours. All of it, and I don't just mean your folks."

It isn't fair for a man to look like Thor and have the sensitivity of Mr. Rogers when dealing with an unreasonably distraught female. Worse, he was right, and I should have said so, but instead, I said, "I just want everything to go right."

"Give me the list."

I hadn't expected that. "The grocery list?

Why?"

Drew shook his head. "Not that one. The menu."

"Why?"

When I hesitated, he snapped his fingers, and I slid across the table the printout of the menu I'd been working from to make the shopping list.

"Okay, then. I'll take a pass on the apple pie because chocolate and pumpkin are more than enough, and I'll make both, so that's entirely off your plate."

My brows shot up so fast I felt a prickle across my forehead. "You bake pies?"

Solemnly, he shook his head. "Nope, but you have a recipe, and a recipe is nothing but a set of instructions. I'm capable of following instructions, so I can handle a couple of pies. You don't have to do everything yourself.”

Since I hadn’t been entirely sure I could handle the pies even with the store-bought crust, I thought he might be getting ahead of himself, but then again, Drew was a force when he put his mind to a task. Still, I sensed there was more to it than that.

“Laudable and appreciated. What’s the rest of it?”

The tips of his ears turned pink, and I knew I was onto something.

“Those store-bought crusts have a weird flavor. I prefer homemade, and again, you don’t have to do everything yourself.”

The lure of that first fight lurked in the dark corners of my psyche, which is the only reason I can think of for flaring up like he’d poured gas on a fire.

“So if I can’t bake a pie the way you prefer,

you'll be forced to step in and do it yourself? Is that what you're saying?" The demon on my left shoulder drowned out the angel on my right.

"No." A stillness settled over him, probably because he didn't dare move for fear of provoking me. "I'm saying you didn't get much notice about this whole Thanksgiving thing, and I can see that you're stressing out over it. The pies are a chore I could take off your shoulders while satisfying my preference for homemade crust. It's sensible."

His reasonable tone ticked me off more. It wasn't like I couldn't see myself being unreasonable. It was more that I couldn't stop poking him, trying to provoke a fight.

"Ah, so it's my parent's fault for taking time to help a friend."

That one caused a tiny spark of annoyance. I watched it flare in his eyes, then go out as he studied me soberly. And that ticked me off even more. How dare he try to understand me. I am woman. A creature of mystery and allure. An unknowable force with depths no mere man could parse.

I am full of crap.

Jane Anderson's call interrupted the tension. I rose and walked out of the kitchen to handle the problem, and by the time I'd agreed to go and see Jamie's latest escapade, Drew had found someplace else to be. I did notice he'd taken the time to cross apple pie off the menu and initial the other two. He'd also crossed the crusts off my shopping list and added a smiley face.

It only made me more annoyed, and I left

without saying goodbye.

"I'm so sorry," Jane Anderson stood in the doorway while I assessed the damage. "I honestly don't know how this happened."

Your son is a menace, is how it happened, I wanted to say, but bit my tongue before the comment popped out. "Well, I appreciate you trying to take care of it on your own."

Several fresh coats of primer hadn't been enough to obliterate little Jamie's artwork, which covered the lower three feet of every wall in his bedroom. In permanent marker of all things.

"Tim Bennett said this stuff should cover it, and it seemed like it did, but after a few hours, the marker seeped through again." Jane rubbed a circle on her forehead and closed her eyes for a moment. I thought she looked weary. "And the smell of it gives me a headache. I don't know what else to do."

"Locking your art supplies away might help for a start." Although my tone was dry, it was dry with humor, not condemnation. Jane let a smile tug the corners of her mouth.

"Already done. Believe me."

At that point, the artist himself strutted down the hallway, and I had to curl my lips under and bite them to hold back a smile. His wall hadn't been his only canvas.

"Look," he held up an arm covered in black squiggles for me to see. "I'm Aquaman. See my tattoos."

"Very nice." My gaze met that of his weary mother, and Jane shook her head in resignation. I hunkered down to Jamie's eye level. "But you shouldn't put tattoos on the walls, okay?"

"Okay." Cheerful, he smiled at me, his face as innocent as a cherub's and twice as cute. "Pick me up." He held up chubby arms, his fingers curling in and out. Then, when I did, he gave me a smacking kiss on the cheek, snuggled up under my chin, and sighed. My heart melted.

"It's a good thing he's cute," his mother said, smiling at my besotted face.

"I think you'll have your hands full with him."

"Already do." Jane gestured to the wall. "I'll pay whatever it costs to fix this, but I have no idea what it needs. It's like the nightmare that just keeps coming back around to spread terror again and again."

My brain kicked in with a possible solution.

"What if you painted the lower half of the wall with chalkboard paint? It comes in black, so it would probably cover the writing and give Jamie a ready-made canvas to draw on."

Jane's eyes lit up. "That's brilliant. And you don't think Leo would mind?"

"If he does, it will be on my head since it was my idea. If that doesn't work, we'll figure something else out."

My phone bonged out my text message tone. Hope hit me for a brief second, then died a painful death when I saw the name, and it wasn't Jacy. I'd stopped answering her texts a few days after the great Jober Peavey debacle, so why did I keep thinking she'd try again? This was the best thing I could do for her. The text being from Delilah heaped punishment on top of pain.

Come to my room. Important.

Like I was on call or something.

Soon as I can.

Out of spite for her assumptive methods, I dawdled a bit on my way out to the Bide-A-Way Motel. Delilah needed to know she couldn't order me around. I might have ridden my high horse to her door, but I don't like thinking about that now.

I knocked. No answer, but her car was out front. What the hell?

I knocked again. "Delilah, are you in there? Open the door."

That's when the worry began to settle in. I gave it one more shot, then headed for the office to get the master key.

"Something's wrong. Delilah messaged me to come over, but she's not answering the door, and I have a bad feeling."

Barbara Dexter, motel owner, wasted no time grabbing her key and following me to unit seven. I knocked once more, waited for an answer that never came, and stepped back to let Barbara fit the key in the lock.

It wasn't good, what was on the other side of the door. I knew that before it swung open.

Delilah sat at the small table near the window, her head slumped forward. I rushed to her side, hunkered down to look at her face. Her eyes, fixed and staring, the silk scarf wrapped around her neck, ends trailing down her back were signs of what I would find when I tested her pulse.

"She's gone," I looked at Barbara and noted her expression mirrored mine: wide eyes and sorrow. "I'll make the call."

Please, I sent up a fervent wish, don't let

Carole Ann be the one who answers.

Wish denied. Carole Ann answered with her usual bored tone.

"What's your emergency?"

I sighed. "I need Ernie out at the Bide-A-Way as soon as he can get here."

"Who's dead?"

What was the sense of dancing around the truth? "Delilah Cannon."

Then, I held the phone away from my ear when she didn't bother to hang up before screeching Ernie's name. "That Everly Dupree's gone and killed someone again. Out at the motel."

"I didn't—" I began.

"Dupree," Ernie came on the line. "Who's dead?"

"Delilah Cannon and I didn't kill her. Carole Ann's an idiot."

136

He neither confirmed nor denied.

"On my way. Don't—"

My turn to cut him off. "I know the drill. I won't touch anything."

I did, however, take a good, long look around and snap a few photos with my phone before I hustled Barbara back out of the room to wait for what came next.

"We really need to stop finding bodies together," Barbara tried for levity in the face of tragedy. "This is the second time, and I have to say, it's getting old."

Nodding ruefully, I couldn't help but wonder, would Delilah still be alive if I'd not dawdled and arrived sooner? The five minutes before Ernie pulled in passed with me contemplating that question and responding to Barbara when every so often, she said, "Isn't this a hell of a thing?"

Funnily enough, Ernie voiced the same sentiment upon his arrival. "Hell of a thing. You really do need to find a new hobby."

I rolled my eyes, which probably wasn't the best response given the day's events. Still, after he instructed Barbara to return to her office until he needed to speak to her, I followed him into the unit anyway. "She texted me about half an hour before I got here, said she needed to see me, and it was important."

All I got was a grunt for a response while Ernie inspected the crime scene.

"When I arrived, she didn't answer the door, so Barbara used her master, and we found her like this. Looks like she's been strangled with her own scarf. Reminds me of how Davina was killed. Do you think the two deaths are related?"

If he didn't, he was an idiot. At least now that the question popped into my head. I missed Ernie's next comment as my mind rolled through the possibilities. In her text, Delilah said it was important that we meet. If her death and Davina's were related, and if she showed up as a ghost—make that when since, given my haunted history, Delilah hanging around on the wrong side of the veil was inevitable—she probably wouldn't be able to tell me why she'd asked to meet. Just peachy.

When I tuned back in, he was saying, "—wait for the autopsy results, but I've had some experience with such things." Ernie broke off to give me a pointed look, which I returned with a narrow-eyed glare. It wasn't my fault I kept stumbling over dead folks. "And given the body temp, I'd say she's been dead for at least two hours.”

“That’s impossible,” I said, pulling out my phone. “She texted me not even an hour ago.”

Ernie’s brows shot up, then dipped back down into a frown. “She’s definitely been dead longer than an hour. You sure the text came from her?”

I flipped the screen around to show him the time and date stamp. “Positive. Find her phone. I’m sure that will confirm it.”

Looking skeptical, he checked near the body, found nothing, so began a systematic search of the dresser drawers, Delilah’s empty suitcase, the nightstand, and the bathroom. “It’s not here.” He even knelt to check under the bed.

“It’s probably in her purse.” I glanced around and didn’t see that, either.

Ernie went back to his car, returning moments later with an extra pair of latex gloves, which he handed to me. "If you won't leave, you might as well make yourself useful. There's a set of car keys on the nightstand. Take them and check her car, but don't—"

"I know. Don't touch anything unless I absolutely have to." I left him with the body and went to do as I was told. I hadn't known Delilah all that well and hadn't been interested in making fast friends with her under any circumstances. Still, I felt horrible about her death and let a few tears fall while I unlocked her car, then checked between and under the seats for her purse.

"Nothing." I went back inside and dropped the keys on the nightstand. "The killer must have taken it with them."

Absently, Ernie nodded. "Probably. What can you tell me about the deceased? Why was she in town? And can you send me a screenshot of the text you received? With the time and date."

I sent the screenshot first, bought myself a little time to decide how much to tell him, then went with the truth. "Delilah came to Mooselick River to write a tell-all book about Davina Benet."

"What all was there to tell?"

"Not much outside of what the public already knew, which is why that was Delilah's cover story. She was really here to see if she could solve Davina's murder. She figured if she told everyone her research was for a book, they'd open up more readily when she asked questions."

"I know how to do my job. I don't need a

bunch of amateur sleuths getting in my way."

We both knew that remark was aimed at me just as much as at Delilah. Maybe it would have been easier to tell him about my ghosts and why I got more involved with his investigations than I should have. But after what had happened with Neena, I couldn't bring myself to do it.

"It's not my intention to get in your way. I seem to have a knack for being in the right place at the right time. Or maybe the wrong place at the wrong time." I frowned and tried again. "Right place, wrong time. I don't know. It's not a reflection of your ability. It's just the luck of the devil, I guess."

"Well, cut it out. I'm following all possible leads, and Davina Benet's murderer will face justice with or without your devilish luck.”

Who was he trying to convince? Himself or me?

“You see what happens to people who stick their noses in police business?” Ernie pointed to Delilah’s body. “Maybe you should mind yours.”

“So you do think the two deaths were related?”

Frowning, Ernie’s face went thunderous. “I didn’t say that. Go home, Everly. If I have more questions, I know where to find you.”

Red lights flashed outside as the ambulance pulled into the space next to my car. Distant sirens announced that more police officers were on their way. At this point, Ernie had made it clear I wouldn’t learn anything new by hanging around, so I honored his request. However, I stopped by the office on my way out to have a word with Barbara, who promised to call me if she heard anything interesting.

"Ernie was right. What's a hobby that doesn't involve dead people?" A resilient woman, Barbara had recovered quickly from the trauma. "How do you feel about bridge?"

"Too complicated. They're offering knitting classes at the new craft shop." I pointed out. Despite the gravity of the day, Barbara barked out a laugh.

"And make pornographic pot picker-uppers? I think I'll pass."

"I hear they're a hit with the tourists."

Barbara laughed again, this time sounding more like herself. Since I didn't want to see them carry the body bag out, I asked if she was okay, and when she said she was, I headed home.

Poor Delilah. Did she have a family? I'd never asked. It hadn't seemed important.

CHAPTER EIGHT

Apparently, the Tuesday afternoon before Thanksgiving was too late to shop for Thanksgiving fixings. Drew hadn't needed to worry about suffering through the iffy flavor of store-bought crust because there wasn't one left in the store. I did manage to snag the last bag of stuffing crumbs and a box of Bell's poultry seasoning, but unless my mother had a can of filling in her cabinets, the hotly contested pumpkin pie wouldn't be on the menu.

Thankfully, they still had plenty of yeast

and butter for the rolls, and I scored on the fresh cranberries, too. I had to find a substitute for brussels sprouts, but they had plenty of squash and sweet potatoes, so long as I didn't want those with tiny marshmallows because that shelf was picked clean.

It came as no surprise to find two ghosts sitting on my front steps when I got home. Nor was I particularly shocked that neither of them looked happy about it—for different reasons, of course.

"Thanks a lot," Delilah shot off her perch and got right up in my face, the chill coming off her making my eyeballs hurt. "Are you happy now that you got me killed?"

I didn't care if Neena looked out her window and saw me talking to no one.

"That's rich." Delilah flinched when I poked

my finger into her chest. Until then, it had never occurred to me that they might find my touch as revolting as I did theirs. "You blaming me for your death. Did I invite you to come and stick your nose into things? No. No, I did not. You did that on your own, so if it got you killed, you only have yourself to blame."

Delilah's fury prickled across my skin.

"Dial it back," I ordered through clenched teeth. "Get some control. I'm going inside. When you're done with," I pointed and circled my hand at her, "all of this attitude, you can come in, and we'll talk. Until then, you're not welcome."

Davina winked at me as I gathered my groceries and passed her on the steps. She knew it wasn't necessary to have my permission to come into the house, but

Delilah didn't. For good effect, I slammed the door behind me. Twenty minutes later, when Drew came home, the house remained ghost free. At least on the inside.

Having followed proper girlfriend etiquette, despite my earlier display of temper, I'd called him as soon as I left the motel but insisted he finish his classes for the day. When he pulled me in, I cradled my head against his chest, listened to the constant thrum of his heart, and felt safe for the first time all day.

"You okay?"

"I am, now." My arms went around his waist as I burrowed closer. He'd showered at the gym and smelled of man and soap and comfort. "We're alone, by the way. For the moment, anyhow. They were outside when I got home, the both of them." I pulled back far enough to reach up and put my palms on his cheeks while I kissed him.

"If that was meant to be a distraction from whatever comes next, I'll take it," He leaned in and returned the favor with heat.

"It's an apology for being hideous to you earlier and a thank you for being there for me now, for being solid even when I've acted a fool. You should probably take this as a warning that with me, things always get weirder before they get better."

Drew kissed me again. "You've got me, and I'm not going anywhere."

Just like that: forgiveness. Whether I deserved it or not. When I said as much, he kissed me again.

"Stress relief. We all have days when we need to release some pressure. Besides, weird is never boring, so I say, bring it." He grinned, then sobered. "Are you sure it's a good idea to pursue Davina's killer? Assuming the two deaths are related, it might not be safe."

"They have to be related. There's no other reason why Delilah would be dead right now because, as much as I hate to admit it, she might have been right. Seems like the killer has to be someone local. Otherwise, how would they know Delilah was here and sniffing around the case?"

"What about someone from outside but with local ties?"

"Possible, but it doesn't ring for me. I need to ask Delilah who knew she'd moved to the Bide-A-Way."

Since Molly was doing her gotta-pee dance, I reluctantly left the safety of Drew's arms and headed toward the back door.

Davina waited on the other side.

"You want to tell me what happened?"

My patience had run out. "What happened? Delilah pried into your murder—you know, the one you're so positive no one had a motive to commit, and now, she's dead. I assumed you could figure that much out on your own."

"Funny," Davina pitched me a dirty look, but it came without the chill of heightened ghostly emotion. "I'm sorry Delilah's dead. Just in case that isn't clear."

"Good of you, I'm sure."

"But I can't help thinking her death is a big fat clue to mine."

I rolled my eyes so hard I almost heard them creak. "Just coming around to having a little common sense, are we?"

"Smartass." The chill of ghostly

displeasure stole over my skin but dissipated quickly. "I see the light."

"Like the one on the other side of the veil? You should go into it."

"Don't give up your day job for a career in comedy," Davina leaned over to bump my shoulder with hers. Didn't go quite as she planned. Felt nasty. "Sorry. I forgot I'm not solid."

"Where's your sidekick?" A glance around didn't turn up Delilah, which was unexpected. "Seems like a golden opportunity for her to get to know the real Davina Benet. Or Lucy Bennett, even."

Davina flicked away the notion. "She talked me into going back to the scene of the crime. Thought it would trigger her memory of the event."

"Ghost go poof?"

Delilah nodded. "Pretty much, but you're wrong. She doesn't want to know the real me. She wants to get closer to the version of me she made up in her head. All-knowing, all-seeing crusader for those who didn't come home."

To my surprise, Davina sounded lonely.

"I get it. I mean, it's not easy when you have something extra. Not everyone will understand. Most people won't, and some are just plain mean. Did you have a good life? Friends? Did you find love?"

These were questions I probably should have asked before. Half the reason I'd been twiddling my thumbs on this investigation was from a lack of personal information. Maybe I'd been trying to get her to tell me the wrong things all along.

"There was someone a few years back. Or

155

I thought there was. It didn't work out," Davina answered the last question first. "Relationships are difficult enough to navigate. When you do what I do…or did, I guess, that adds a whole other dimension to things. You can't always count on people."

"Preaching to the choir, but I got lucky in that department." Even if we still hadn't had that first fight.

"I learned my lesson early on about getting involved with anyone connected to one of my cases, but there were men when I wanted them. Work took up most of my time, so I looked for fulfillment there. And the travel is a nice side perk if you can get it. I kept in touch with Leandra, who is as true a friend as one could ask for."

She'd loosened up a little, so I scooted back inside for a jacket, then tossed a rubber flying disc for Molly. "What's the weirdest thing anyone ever asked you to find?"

"My agent tried to get me to commit to a publicity stunt where I found a needle in an actual haystack. I had to pass on that one, but the weirdest thing had to be—" Davina broke off, then grinned and continued, "You know, I don't usually talk about the stranger aspects of my work because I have to normalize it to keep from scaring most people off, but I think you might understand."

I held up my hand. "The ghost of my high school sweetheart rolled a mannequin head down my stairs to knock out his killer, who was trying to strangle me at the time. That was my introduction to the land of the weird."

When Davina began to speak, I shook my head to stop her. "Then, my former boss was crushed to death by a stack of recycled paper because the woman he got his dog from didn't like his training methods. When we went to talk to her, she tried to toss my best friend and me off a cliff. We had to have ghostly help for that one, too."

"Okay. You get it."

"I know our gifts aren't exactly the same, but we probably have more in common than you think." Maybe finding that common ground was the way to get her to show me the breadcrumbs I'd need to follow to find her killer. "So, the weirdest thing?"

"Had to be a toilet seat cover."

Okay, I wasn't expecting that. "Come again?"

"You heard me right. An autographed toilet

seat cover."

"You mean like one of those slip-on cloth things or an actual toilet seat lid? I think I need the whole story."

"The actual lid. Autographed to his college roommate by a budding movie star who ended up becoming a very big deal. The lid went missing—lost when the owner moved houses. Or not lost so much as packed in a box of childhood mementos, probably by the owner's new wife who didn't think a toilet seat lid went with her decorating scheme no matter how nicely it had been framed."

Probably not pertinent to Davina's death, but a really good story.

"So it wasn't all abductions and runaways."

Davina shrugged. "Those were the cases that got people's attention, but there was just as much satisfaction in finding someone's lost wedding ring or a photo album that meant a lot to them. Even the toilet seat lid. I liked helping people."

"No, I get that because I feel the same, even if I do what I do partly to get ghosts out of my house. Even if it cost me a friend, I guess." The corner of Neena's garage roof was just visible from where we sat.

Shifting over a bit, Davina turned to face me so her next statement would hold more weight. "It's not easy having these gifts. People, even friends, don't understand how it pulls at you all the time…the responsibility of being able to see or know things they don't, I mean."

I nodded. "I think it's easier for me because while I've seen more of them than I ever expected, murders don't happen every day."

Davina echoed my nod. "But people and things get lost all the time, and the stories of loss are heartbreaking. Some of them stick with you."

"Which ones stuck with you?"

Countering with a question of her own, Davina asked, "Do you know how many abductions occur within families? And I don't just mean custodial parenting situations, but actual kidnappings with ransom demands or worse."

I admitted I wasn't up on that particular statistic.

"My first official case, an uncle snatched his niece. I told the authorities how to find her before it got to the ransom stage, but he'd had time to begin indoctrinating her. She begged to stay with him and cried when they took him away. That one left a mark on me."

If I could have, I'd have patted her hand or given her a hug to help ease the pain I heard in her voice. "You did the right thing. You saved that poor girl from who knows what."

"I hope so."

"You were a good person," I said, and when Davina shot me a crooked smile, I amended, "You're still a good person. Delilah will figure it out, or maybe you can talk her into crossing over and give us both a break from her until it's your turn."

"Eternity sounds somewhat less appealing with the chance of Delilah dogging my every step."

"Davina, I hope you take this in the way it was intended. I'll help figure out who killed you, which should free you up for crossing over, but if you choose to stay, you need to forget where I live. I mean, you don't have to go home, but you can't stay here."

She grinned. "Deal. And I don't blame you. If I had a man like yours around, I wouldn't want anyone horning in on my time, either."

And just like that, she made me blush. Not that it was that big of a feat. Happened all the time.

"Yes, well. Speaking of Drew, I picked a fight earlier, and he acted like it was nothing. I'm cooking him my version of a Thanksgiving dinner tomorrow, so I've got some prep work to do today. My mom left me some recipes, but not the one for her stuffing, so I'll have to work with what I found at the store, or the whole meal is ruined."

"Pfft."

I didn't think ghosts could blow a raspberry because they don't actually breathe, but Davina did, so I guess you learn something new every day.

"My aunt Polly made the best stuffing," Davina continued. "I have her recipe memorized. If you like, I'll pass it on to you. I know you'll love it. Everyone does."

Since I felt bad that Davina had led a lonely life, I guessed I could be charitable and do some cooking together. It could be fun until Delilah pulled herself back together and showed up to ruin things.

"That sounds wonderful. I hope I have the ingredients on hand. The grocery store looked like it had been through the wars when I stopped there on my way home."

Davina named off what I'd need ending with, "The secret ingredient is saltine crackers."

"Will those little oyster type work?"

"Perfectly."

Since I did have all of the ingredients, and according to Davina, the stuffing flavors would "marry" better if made two days before, we went inside to cook and take my mind off the sight of death. Plus, she wasn't wrong about the stuffing. Better than my mom's.

CHAPTER NINE

At loose ends, I decided to go to the diner for breakfast the next morning—the day before Thanksgiving. With the shop open, it was unlikely I'd run into Neena, and with mostly ghostly companions of late, I needed to be among people.

Alone, I took a stool at the end of the counter where Mabel waited on me herself since Thea was busy with a family at one of the booths.

"Loaded omelet?" Mabel took one look at my face and knew I needed comfort food.

I nodded. "With bacon, a side of home fries, toast, and coffee."

"Somebody had a bad day." I like my diner food but don't normally eat bacon and home fries with my eggs.

"Yesterday. It was the worst."

It didn't take her long to put the plate together, and since I'd waited until after her normal rush, Mabel had some downtime, so she settled on the stool next to me. It creaked under her solid frame.

"Did you really find that woman out at the hotel?" Mabel liked a good piece of gossip but could keep a secret as if she were a vault. "Everyone was talking about it this morning."

Before I could answer, the mother of the family in the booth began to bark orders with all the tender mercy of a drill sergeant. As one, we turned to watch the dance of getting into coats, gathering up a stuffed animal or two, and a seemingly chaotic but oddly organized exodus out the door.

The quiet that came after seemed almost oppressive but didn't last long because Thea broke it by saying, "I saw her, you know. The dead woman. Not too long before it happened, I think."

"Where? How? Was she alone?"

I lined a diagonally-sliced piece of toast with bacon, topped that with a chunk of omelet, and then another layer of bacon before slapping the second half of the toast on top. When Thea shot up an eyebrow, I returned the look, held her gaze deliberately, and took a big bite. If she said one word about eternity or my hips, she'd be wearing those eggs for a hat. I'd had a lousy few weeks and didn't need unwelcome advice on my eating habits.

For once, Thea read the room and kept her trap shut other than to answer the questions I'd asked. "Here. She called in for the lunch special. Roast beef on rye with chips and pickles on the side. She wanted extra of both and paid with her debit card. She was alone as far as I could tell, but it was busy, and I didn't exactly follow her out to her car to check. How was I supposed to know she'd end up dead?"

"You couldn't, but this is really helpful information." I didn't remember seeing a takeout bag in the room or Delilah's car, and I didn't want to look at the crime scene photos in front of Thea and Mabel, so I filed that away for later. "Can you pinpoint the time? And did she say anything that might help us track her movements that day?"

Thea began to answer, but Mabel cautioned, "Take a minute to think, Thea. It's important to get the details right."

"It's okay. I don't need a minute. I'm not sure what time it was, but she mentioned that she'd just moved her things to the motel and asked if we deliver that far."

While Thea spoke, Mabel rose and went over to tap a few buttons on the credit card reader, which spit out a longish slip of paper.

"You got a general idea of when she was in here? I can probably pinpoint the transaction, and there'd be a time-stamp to nail it down exactly."

"It was a little after one when she texted me and asked me to meet her at the motel, and the text made it sound like she was already there. Thea said it was busy here, so probably during or at the end of your lunch rush, right?" I turned to Thea for confirmation.

"That sounds about right."

Narrowing it down, Mabel ripped off both ends of the long strip of paper, leaving the middle section intact. "Lunch special and a drink?" She glanced at Thea for confirmation and received a nod.

"Medium and I charged her fifty cents for the extra chips and pickles."

Mabel only said Thea's name but in her most disapproving voice.

"Well, you shouldn't give away the store. She wanted extra, she paid for extra, and she didn't add a tip, either."

"We'll talk about that later," Mabel promised as she scanned what was left of the slip. "Got it. Lunch special with drink plus tax with extra chips and no tip comes to ten dollars, seventy-six cents." She picked up a pen and circled one of the transactions. "Time-stamp says she was here at 12:38. Does that help?"

"Tells me the prices here are too low," Thea muttered, then put a lid on it when Mabel stared her down. "Whatever. It's your business."

"You'd do well to remember that."

Out of the corner of my eye, I caught Thea making a face when Mabel turned away, then we all turned toward the door when the bell went off.

"Hey, Ernie. How's things?" Mabel pushed off the counter and headed toward the kitchen. "What will it be today? Ham and Swiss? I got a shipment of that Virginia baked you like so much."

"Works for me," Ernie headed over to take the stool next to mine. Great. I guessed we'd be talking about Delilah some more. "Dupree."

"Polk." I almost asked him how they were hanging, then realized I didn't want to know, and we weren't that good friends anyway. But I grabbed the slip from where Mabel had left it near my plate and passed it to him. "The circled transaction is from when Delilah bought lunch here just before her death. She got the daily special with extra chips and pickles and a drink."

His brows went up as he looked at the time on the slip, then he frowned.

"Yeah, I know what you're thinking," I said. "I don't remember seeing a takeout bag or cup in her room. There wasn't anything in the car when I searched for her purse, either, so did she go somewhere else first? Did her killer take her lunch? Where's her purse? And most importantly, did the killer take her phone?"

When Mabel returned with his sandwich, Ernie thanked her politely, then turned to me again. "Killing's bad enough, but stealing someone's lunch afterward is just…it's particularly cold-blooded."

"That's my take as well," I said, thinking how odd it was to talk shop with a cop. Or something of that nature, anyway. "I think we're looking for a sociopath."

"We?" Ernie shot me a sideways look.

"You. Whatever. I'm not trying to horn in on your investigation."

Ernie spun his stool enough to give me a full-on look. "Mabel, I think you'd better call

911 and tell them we've got us a major pants fire here at the diner."

"Ha. Ha. Ha." I injected a dose of scorn into my tone and rolled my eyes to ensure I got my point across. "Any leads, though?"

"Too soon to tell. Waiting on forensics, which will give us stomach contents to put the lunch question to bed, and we'll also see if they recovered skin cells from the murder weapon. I don't expect them to find much because I think our killer used gloves."

"Both times." I didn't make it a question.

"Plenty of news coverage thanks to Baxter pulling his disappearing act so close to Davina's death." Ernie added enough mustard to his sandwich that the sharp scent made my eyes water. "Could be a copycat."

I propped my elbow on the table, leaned

my head in my hand, and looked at him to see if he was putting me on. "What are the chances of that?"

Ernie took a bite, chewed, and talked at the same time. "Somewhere between jack and sh—"

Mabel practically growled at him, and he chose a different word. "Slim." He set the sandwich down, swallowed, then said, "Delilah's father made arrangements to have her body sent back home for the funeral. He drove up to handle it in person, so I had a chance to ask a few questions, and I'll follow through, but I'm not looking in that direction."

"You're looking at her connection to Davina."

He went back to his lunch, but Ernie's thinking and mine meshed on that point.

Whoever killed Delilah had also killed Davina. Solve one, solve the other. He knew it. I knew it. The killer had to know it, and they'd been very careful or very lucky both times. Going back, I picked up on the thread of the earlier conversation.

"Gloves would explain why Patrea's and Davina's were the only fingerprints found on the necklace."

But Ernie shook his head. "Not Davina's. Only Patrea's and only a partial. The individual beads were too small and irregular to hold a full print."

"Really? I'd think if she was wearing the necklace, Davina's fingerprints would have to be on it. You have to touch a necklace to put it on, so there should have been prints. Even partials, like you said. Don't you think not finding any is weird?"

According to Davina, she'd been pricing necklaces when Patrea showed up. Hard to put price tags on items without touching them. I filed the nugget away and would see if I could pry more information out of Davina the next chance I got.

"Who said she was wearing it before the killer arrived? It could have been sitting on the counter where Patrea put it after she picked it up. The killer could have grabbed it on the way past, and it all went down like this."

Ernie mimed picking up something from beside his plate, reached toward me, and pretended to choke me to death while I tried to remember if Davina had said she was wearing the necklace. Maybe I'd just assumed she was.

Did it matter? I wasn't sure, but I added

the fact to my mental file on the case just the same. Ernie might have to wait for the forensic team's report, but I could ask Delilah about her lunch and Davina about the necklace by the end of the day.

"I've got Carole Ann combing through Davina's most recent missing persons cases. She's turned up a couple of people who weren't happy with her performance."

I'd just taken a sip of my drink and only kept from doing a spit take by sucking in a breath at the last minute. Instead of shooting out my mouth, the soda burned a path up my nose.

"Carole Ann?" I sputtered. "I thought she only answered phones."

"I'm short-staffed this close to the holiday, and she's not as dumb as she seems."

"Okay." I didn't argue, but I wanted to.

I also wanted to get a few things prepped ahead of time so my Thanksgiving dinner would go off without a hitch, and I had plenty of new information to mull over. I left Thea a generous tip since she'd been so helpful and took my leave.

CHAPTER TEN

I met David at the door and pulled him back outside for a quick chat on the porch.

"There's been a development."

"I know. I heard about the dead woman already. This is a small town. News travels fast." He handed me a bottle of wine.

Impatient, I motioned for him to stop talking. "No, I mean on the Thanksgiving front. We've got extra guests today. Two of them."

David frowned. "Drew's buddies in town?"

He wouldn't find that prospect daunting as

he'd met several of Drew's friends during the search for Baxter Thomas, a missing older man who had turned out to be a drug trafficking jerk-weasel.

"Not exactly. This would be some friends from my side of things, but you don't have to worry about them hogging all the stuffing. They won't be eating."

Not being an idiot, David clued right in.

"We're having ghosts for Thanksgiving?" He didn't let his face give away his thoughts.

"You make it sound like we'll be eating them for dinner." I tried to lighten the mood.

"I'd rather not if it's all the same to you. Will I be able to see them?"

I nodded.

"Are you freaked out? I can probably do something about it if you are. It's just that it's the year of the misfits, I guess. I'm barely talking to Jacy and definitely not talking to Neena. Patrea will be with Chris and his family, mine with yours, and Drew's folks are also out of town, leaving us three for dinner. I figured it would be fine if the ghosts come for a bit."

David grinned. "Should I be offended you lumped me in with the misfits?"

"Your choice, I guess. You say the word, and I'll bounce the ghosts right out of here. Otherwise, why don't we go in and see if I've managed to do my mother proud with the biggest turkey on the planet?"

"Good thing Nanette turned down my offer to come with. I didn't know about the ghosts, but I didn't think you'd mind if I invited her. Could have been awkward." An understatement delivered in laughing tones.

"If I hadn't been caught up in my own

drama, I'd have invited her myself. Jason, too, and the ghosts would have found somewhere else to be."

Smiling, David said, "Jason will be eating with Thea Lombardi. I think he's halfway in love with her kid."

"But not her?" A tidbit of gossip makes for a good appetizer.

"Maybe," he said, shrugging. "We didn't talk about romance, only turkey plans."

Still, it bothered me to think of Nanette sitting alone. I suggested he call her and press a bit harder for her to come.

"Can't. She turned me down because she had somewhere else to go. Left at five this morning and won't be back until late tomorrow night. I didn't pry, but it sounded like she was meeting family somewhere."

"Okay. I guess we're all set, then." I turned

to open the door, but David grabbed my arm.

"Is there anything I need to know before we go in? Like, is there a special protocol for dealing with ghosts?"

"They'll run out of energy and be gone long before we get to the pumpkin pie—which Drew made from scratch. Don't ask about their killers unless you want them to leave and make your skin crawl on their way out. That's it. They're just people. Recently-dead people."

Seeming to gear himself up, David nodded. "Let's do this, then."

"Okay," I opened the door, then turned back, "one more thing. You don't want to touch them."

"Why not? Does it make them mad?"

"No, it's just the creepiest feeling. Trust

me. You don't want to touch them."

But he looked skeptical, and I could see he wanted to touch a ghost. The impulse probably came from the same one that leads people to inhale when someone else smells something bad. He had to see for himself and would, I was betting, before the meal ended, find a way to touch a ghost.

He couldn't say he hadn't been warned, and since he had, I felt fully justified in planning to enjoy the results.

"Okay, let's do this." Eyes wide, David followed me back inside. We followed laughing voices to the kitchen.

"David's here." He handled the chorus of greetings well enough, relaxing slightly.

I'd left Drew peeling potatoes and realized I hadn't told him how many. He'd done the entire five-pound bag but looked so pleased with himself that I didn't criticize and put them on to cook. We'd be eating hash with our breakfast for a week.

"What can I do to help?" David took in the relatively peaceful scene in the kitchen. Once I'd banished all traces of snit from my arsenal, Drew and I decided to work together. He'd made pies the night before, I'd raided Catherine's stash of electric crockpots to keep everything warm, and the house smelled like turkey.

"You could open that bottle of wine. I know I could go for a glass right now."

He did as I asked, but his eyes kept tracking back to the pair of ghosts. He'd either get used to them or he wouldn't.

"I'd kill for a bite of that pie right now," Delilah said, her face appearing at my shoulder when I opened the refrigerator to pull out a pound of butter. "With whipped cream and a dusting of cinnamon on top. That's how my mother always serves it."

I weighed the idea of telling her Davina could show her how to travel home for the day against using the opening she'd offered me to pry into the details around her death. Then, I decided I could do both. Pry first, offer the chance to be with family after.

"I was at the diner yesterday morning, and Thea mentioned seeing you there not too long before you…uh…before it happened. You bought food."

Delilah snapped her fingers, which didn't make a sound. Odd. "That's right. I'd forgotten." She narrowed her eyes while poring over the memory. "I remember now. I slept in because my alarm didn't go off, so I'd missed breakfast. Then, I packed and paid my bill before going to the motel and settling in."

Having seen what little was in the room, I figured that chore hadn't taken long.

"I stopped at the hardware store to chat with Davina's brother. Didn't learn a thing about her death."

"Who knew you would be at the motel?"

To her credit, she took a moment to think that one through. "David Barrington, obviously, and the rest of the Marlow's staff. The woman who runs the motel."

Impatient, I stuffed down the impulse to remind her I already knew about Barbara.

"I mentioned it to Davina's brother and again at the diner when I stopped to order lunch."

She confirmed what Thea had told me.

"Anyone else? What about after you left

the diner? Or did you go back to the motel?" I watched her carefully for signs of death poofage.

"I can't remember," Delilah shivered.

"Never mind. Don't think about it anymore, okay?"

"Why are you asking?" Davina nosed into the conversation.

"We didn't find any evidence of Delilah having eaten lunch at the motel after, well, you know," I admitted. "But we'll talk about all of this later. Right now, I have to get these rolls in the oven."

A tea towel covered a pan of rising bread that looked almost like my mom's. If the turkey tasted as good as it smelled, I'd definitely done her proud.

It took a concerted effort on Drew's and my part, with a little help from David, but we got everything into serving dishes and on the table while it was all still hot. The meal went far better than I expected, and Drew's pies were top-notch, given his amateur baker status.

"Can I ask you a favor?" David had stayed behind to help me clean up while Drew went to the living room to turn on the TV and check football scores. "It's okay if you say no."

"I probably won't."

"You might because it's a tricky subject, and I almost hate to bring it up." He slung the dishtowel over his shoulder. "It's just that I know Neena is home alone today."

I held out a hand, "Stop right there. I've got no problem with Neena. She has one with me, so if you think you can broker peace, I'm already on board, but you won't get anywhere with her. I never wanted it to be like this."

"I know." David reached over and squeezed my shoulder. "I may not be the most socially astute man you'll ever meet, but even I am not stupid enough to get in the middle between two women. I just wanted to know if it was okay if I made her a plate and took it over."

My heart headed for my feet, taking my stomach along for the ride. "I figured she'd go to the Montayne's." I handed him the newly-scrubbed turkey pan to dry while visions of Neena sitting alone in the dark played across my mind. No matter what, I didn't want that for her.

"That was the plan right up until Viola called her last night to say she'd decided not to observe the holiday this year on account of cruelty to poultry. They had Thanksgiving breakfast instead. Oatmeal with cranberries in it."

"Seems about right for Viola. I'm sure Neena could have gone to Jacy's."

"Jacy and Brian were eating with Brian's folks this year."

Feeling completely out of the loop, I began to fill a plate. "Tell her…never mind." I wanted him to tell her I missed her, but I didn't want to come off as either desperate or pushy.

Food is love. Or so it's said. Leaning into the platitude, I'd let the food do my talking for me and tucked two slices of pie in a plastic storage dish to go along with the generous plate I'd wrapped in foil.

"Here. That should do it." I popped everything in an insulated bag and sent

David off with my blessing. "Take your time over there. No one should be alone on Thanksgiving."

After he'd gone, I gave in to misery and allowed a few tears to fall before I joined Drew on the sofa and let the sounds of the game wash over me. Football wasn't my thing, but I'd made the man eat dinner with a pair of chatty ghosts. Relationships require give and take on all sorts of funny levels.

CHAPTER ELEVEN

The thing about small towns is that you can't avoid people forever. Or even for long. Case in point, I ran into Jacy and Leandra in the parking lot of the Gas-N-Go on my way to help Patrea at the flip house the Friday after Thanksgiving. It did not go well. At least, not at first.

I'd just finished filling my tank when I turned around to see two women, arms crossed and glaring at me.

Given the circumstances, there was probably a right thing to say. Something grave and full of emotional weight. Like, I'm sorry, or I was an idiot, please forgive me, or how have you been, even. Something good and decent.

What came out of my mouth was not at all the right thing. "Jeez, Jace, you look more and more like your mother every day." Or maybe it was the right thing if I had intended to piss them both off, which was already the case, so it was a wasted effort.

"My, my." Jacy turned to Momma Wade. "Do you see what I see? I think it's Mooselick River's latest tragedy. Lost when she declared herself dead to all those who loved her, it's the ghost of Everly Dupree."

Leandra, of course, went right along with her daughter. "Are you sure? I thought she only committed social suicide."

"Ouch. That was harsh," I muttered and

came out with the apology I should have kicked off with. Heartfelt as they were, Jacy wasn't moved by my words. She maintained her folded-arms stance and quirked a brow.

"I get why you're mad," I said. "I really do."

"Is that so? I'd like to know how you think you understand how it feels to be ghosted by your best friend." Jacy's chin jutted out stubbornly. "For the second time."

I might have underestimated just how much trouble I was in.

"I've never ghosted you," Jacy pointed out. "Never. And I never would, so tell me how you think it feels, why don't you?"

At some point, Momma Wade had quietly moved out of the line of fire. Maybe she wanted to give us a minute to work things out, or maybe she was similarly annoyed and didn't want to gang up on me.

When tears threatened, I blinked them back, knowing that if Jacy saw them, she was too soft-hearted to stay mad. I couldn't afford to let her see me cry. She might feel manipulated, and if we were to salvage our relationship, I needed to get closer to solid ground without playing on her temperament.

Not that I had the least clue how to do that as the standoff wore on.

"I was just trying to protect you," I finally muttered. In retrospect, I can see there was no right thing to say.

Jacy added a toe-tap to the crossed arms and quirked eyebrow. "Really? From what? Being dumped by a friend? Oh, wait. Can you actually protect someone from a thing by doing that thing? I can never tell."

"I didn't want to force you to take sides in this break with Neena. I didn't want to put you in the middle or hurt your business. I thought it would be easier for you this way. Then you wouldn't have to decide between two people you cared about."

"You're an idiot." But I could see she'd softened slightly. Jacy is the most decent person I know. She doesn't hold grudges and is always willing to look at both sides of a problem. "But I guess I can see your thinking. It doesn't make it right, and I think I will require a boon to reinstate you as my best friend."

"A boon?"

"Yes, but I haven't decided what it will be, so you'll just have to wait until I do." She held out her arms so we could hug it out. I moved into them without hesitation. She squeezed me and then whispered in my ear, "If you ever ghost me again, it had better be because you're actually dead. You get me?"

The hug ended abruptly when we heard applause. As one, we turned to see both Gas-N-Go workers standing out front with Leandra.

Jacy giggled, then hugged me again.

"That," she said, "is a testament to the fact we need more entertainment in this town."

Having left the audience of three, Leandra walked over, gave me a mock glare, then hugged me nearly as hard as her daughter had. "Come visit me at the bookstore soon, okay? I've missed you, too."

Too choked up to speak properly, I nodded and cleared my throat. "I will."

"But you won't come by the shop, will you?" Maybe things weren't as rosy with Jacy as they'd seemed. "Because of Neena."

I shrugged. "It wouldn't be fair to her If I showed up and made her uncomfortable in her place of business. It's bad enough that we live across the street from each other."

"She says she hardly ever sees you outside," Jacy said.

Again, I shrugged. "This is what I'm talking about. I don't want to know what she says about me, and I don't want to put you in the middle. The topic of Neena has to be off the table because I won't jeopardize what you're building with her. I care too much about you both to be the cause of that."

"You're a pair of idiots," was Jacy's last word on the subject. "I'm already in the middle, and there's nothing you can do about it. I ought to lock the both of you in a room together until you figure things out."

"Probably." I couldn't deny I felt better for

having this all too public confrontation. "But I'd rather you didn't, and I'm sure she would, too."

"Fine. I'll leave it alone, but only if you agree not to freeze me out again."

"I won't."

"Good because my inventory of second chances is running low. You and Neena need to get your poop in a group soon. I want everything to go back to normal."

"I'm not sure I'd recognize normal if it walked up and kicked me in the shins," I muttered to Jacy's retreating back.

"I heard that," she tossed over her shoulder. "Just get it done."

CHAPTER TWELVE

"About time you got here." Patrea whipped the door open before I could knock. "I've got something to show you."

I followed her inside, expecting to learn the finer points of applying a French polish, or maybe she'd found another secret cupboard. Not that the last one had offered anything interesting. Instead, Patrea led me upstairs to the attic space where she'd set up a murder board with photos of Davina and Delilah: notes and clippings about each woman with several red strings stretched between those in patterns that didn't make sense to me at first glance.

"It's not done, obviously." Patrea watched my face for signs of what I thought of her handiwork. "But I thought a visual representation of the facts might help nail down our suspects."

I walked closer, saw she'd pinned strips of blank paper to the lower left-hand corner, and hung a marker from one of the red strings.

"Here at the top, I've put Davina on the left, Delilah on the right," Patrea explained her system. "The red string represents the timeline for both murders, and I figured we could write the suspect's names on those pieces of paper, tack them along the bottom, and then use this to make connections between them." She produced a ball of blue string. "Maybe we'll see a pattern emerge."

"I've been spinning my wheels so long with this one, I'm willing to try anything. Davina has finally realized she made an enemy but can't think of who it could be. We all agree that whoever killed one woman also killed the other. Delilah's certain it's someone who lives in town, but I think the answer lies in Davina's past cases."

"What if you're both right?"

I frowned since I hadn't considered that angle before. "Don't you think Davina would know if she'd run into someone from her hometown when she was elsewhere? Or if someone from here carried that big of a grudge? I'd have thought she'd pick right up on that. Open and shut."

Or not.

"I meant, what if someone from Davina's past, someone who had something to do with one of her cases, moved here recently."

Why didn't I think of that before?

"We have had a few transplants over the past few months. I figured they resulted from Martha's tireless efforts to bring attention, but you're absolutely right. Someone connected to her could have moved to town, and now, I wish Davina was here. I have questions."

"She's not?" Patrea glanced around just in case the ghost was standing right behind her. "I'm not sure how all of that works, but if you want to call her, it's okay with me."

"They mostly just show up whenever they want." Whether I liked it or not. "But sometimes they come if I call them. Here goes." I raised my voice. "Davina. Can you hear me?"

"That's lame," Patrea muttered.

"What? Were you expecting me to whip out a crystal ball or a scrying mirror?"

"No, I guess not. But how cool would it be if you had a crystal ball?"

"She'd probably drop it on her foot," Davina spoke to Patrea, not to me. Patrea's eyes went a little wide, but even so, she grinned.

"You're probably right."

"Thanks for the less-than-stellar assessment," I said without heat. "I'm not that clumsy."

"Yes, you are," Davina and Patrea spoke in unison, but the moment served to release the last of Patrea's nerves so I didn't waste time arguing the point.

"We've had a thought on your case," I

said, drawing Davina's attention to the board. "Patrea set this up."

"I'd have done it better." Delilah popped up nearby.

"Really?" I grabbed the ball of blue string and tossed it at the ghost, who reached out, then glared at me as the string passed right through her.

Patrea sucked in a breath, let it out on a sigh, shook her head, and said to me, "You get used to this type of thing, right?"

"Eventually," I said, my voice as dry as winter air. "Takes practice and a certain level of tolerance. Mine isn't as strong as it used to be."

"Did you call us here for a reason?" Delilah glared at me.

Technically, I hadn't called her there at all, so I turned to Davina. "Does the name

Jason Todd mean anything to you? Or Nanette Hill?" I ran through the first two names that came to mind.

Davina shrugged. "Not in the context you're asking about, no. I'm aware they both work at the Marlow and that Jason makes the most divine pastries. I spent a night at the inn waiting for the movers to deliver my things."

"No spark there?"

Confusion tugged a frown across Davina's face. "Spark? Um, no. He's young enough to be my son. What kind of cougar do you think I am?"

My frown matched hers before the mental image hit. "Ew, no. I meant psychically. Like, did either spark anything to do with your finding-people talent."

When I glanced over, I saw that Patrea

had curled her lips under to keep from smiling.

"Oh." All business now, Davina paused to think, then shook her head. "Not in that way, no. I don't remember speaking to either of them. I arrived late in the day, as I recall. The nice young man who owns the inn offered to raid the kitchen and send up a selection of pastries since they don't offer room service, as such."

Davina's voice went all soft and reverent. "Best cream horn I've ever eaten. Buttery, sweet pastry with a silky, smooth custard filling." Her eyes closed as she relived the experience, then opened again to meet mine. "I ate, drank a cup of tea, and went to bed early because I had to be at the house at eight to meet the movers. I checked out and left by seven."

Going into cross-examination mode, Patrea asked a few follow-up questions, which elicited the same answers. No, Davina hadn't met Jason or Nanette after her night at the inn. No, she hadn't run into anyone she recognized from her past. No, she hadn't kept track of people connected to her cases unless they'd made contact. No, she hadn't felt any psychic tingle.

"It doesn't work like that," Davina said. "Not for me, anyway. Not out of the blue. Are we done here?"

"Not yet," I said as another name popped to the surface. "Did you ever meet a woman named Megan McCurdy?" Megan had moved to the area around the same time as Davina and had been involved in her fair share of scandal.

"Doesn't ring a bell."

"She worked at the assisted living facility when Baxter Thomas went missing." I described her to Davina.

A moment passed while Davina considered.

"The abrasive know-it-all?"

"That'd be the one," I said and suppressed a smile since that's how I thought of her, too. "Any contact with her while you were still among the living?"

"Not really." Davina shook her head. "I mean, nothing of a personal nature. I may have spoken to her in passing when I went out to help with the search, but I can't say for sure."

I turned to Delilah. "What about you?"

She shook her head. "Never heard of her."

"As usual, you've been a world of help." I barely kept the sarcasm out of my voice.

"You're welcome. Call on me anytime." Davina faded away, taking Delilah with her.

"I don't recall thanking her, but I should have known she's be as helpful as snowshoes on the beach."

Patrea grabbed my hand, and I felt hers tremble. "Do you know what just happened?"

"Uh, yeah. Davina was her usual self and gave no useful information."

If she heard me, I couldn't tell. "I just spoke to not one, but two ghosts. They were right there," she said, pointing to the spot where Davina had been.

"I know."

"That's huge."

I shrugged. "We didn't learn anything, so I think huge might be an overstatement."

"Didn't we?"

"Not unless you count the knowledge that Jason makes orgasmic pastry, which wasn't exactly news to me."

It's rare to hear Patrea giggle, but she did. "I don't recall Davina mentioning the word orgasmic."

Grinning back, I said, "She didn't have to. I've had one of those cream horns."

"Killer cream horns. Or better yet, if he turns out to be the murderer, we could call him the Cream Horn Killer."

Granted, I hadn't known Jason very long and didn't know him very well, but I hoped he wasn't the killer. It would be a shame to send a culinary genius to jail. I would if I had to, but I'd regret it. Still, I picked up the pen, added his name to one of the slips of paper, and pinned it to the board. Nanette's followed, and then Megan's.

Head tilted, Patrea surveyed the results. She retrieved the ball of blue string, cut two pieces, and pinned both to Jason's name tag. "One for Davina, one for Delilah since they both stayed at the inn." She did the same for Nanette's name, then stood back to survey the results. "I'm not sure what to put for Megan unless you somehow think the thing with Baxter was related to Davina's death."

"We ruled that out at the time, but this is a start," I said when neither of us suffered any sort of epiphany. "Now, we ask around to see if anyone else moved to town during the time in question, and we look a little harder at Jason and Nanette, I guess. Megan, too."

Having stood back to analyze the board, Patrea crossed her arms. "First, we should define the time in question, don't you think?

Jason and Nanette arrived ahead of Davina moving back to town. We know this because the inn was open, and Davina stayed there, which begs the question: when did Davina decide to come home, and if one of these two is the killer, how did they learn about her plans? Also, do we know when Megan moved to town?"

I didn't have an answer. "Pinning down the sequence of events pertains even if it wasn't Jason or Nanette. If we're on the right track, the killer was in place ahead of time, which speaks to a higher level of premeditation than I'd thought. Something precipitated the killer to choose this time and place, but, and I'm certain of this much, Davina has no idea what that something might have been."

"Or she refuses to see," Patrea observed.

"True," I agreed. "Can you blame her?"

"Why can't she just tell you what happened?" The question made me realize I hadn't told Patrea all the details about how things worked.

"Because that would be too easy, and we can't have that." Sarcasm made my point for me. "They're apparently not allowed. Maybe it's too traumatic. I don't know. All I know is if I ask questions that come too close to them giving me anything concrete, they freak out and go poof on me."

"Okay, we can work with that," Patrea's eyes glittered as she turned to me. "Unless you have something against freaking them out on purpose. Can't we do a lineup and see which person makes Davina go poof?"

"Again, that would be too easy. Remember the bowling for murderers story? I'm exceedingly grateful that Hudson had no problem being in the room with his killer. So proximity isn't enough."

I hadn't even finished before Patrea was shaking her head. "You'd already figured out who it was when Hudson showed up. Am I right?"

"Well, yeah. I guess so."

"Which means there's a distinction between proximity and informational exchange."

She was making my head hurt, but her analysis of the situation was spot on, and I could almost see where she was going. "I guess so," I repeated, "but we just discussed three possible suspects with Davina, and she didn't so much as quiver, so I'm not sure how to turn her response to our advantage without first knowing who the murderer was."

Crestfallen, Patrea abandoned that line of thinking. Probably not permanently, but for the time being, anyway. "It feels like a start. Next step, I guess, we ask around about new arrivals during the murder windows. We just need to define the parameters."

Her approach made sense to me. "I have to figure we look at when Davina decided to move back home. When and to whom she announced that decision, too, since it seems like the killer may have anticipated and arrived ahead of time. Or do we cross-check with anyone who knew Delilah was moving to the motel?"

"Good point. I say we do both. Widen the scope, so we don't miss anyone, then narrow it down. To that end, we must also consider anyone who visited family during the murder window."

Davina's murder coincided with a search for a missing man, bringing a crowd to town to help find him. Talk about a needle in a haystack. We needed someone with Davina's talent. Too bad she couldn't use it from beyond the grave.

Still, with a rudimentary plan for moving forward, we tabled further death discussion until after the holiday.

CHAPTER THIRTEEN

"Where is everyone?" Martha sat alone in the town office when I arrived for our scheduled planning meeting. "Am I really early? That hardly ever happens."

"You're not early. No one else is coming." Behind newish bifocals, Martha's gaze spelled ruin for anyone who dared duck out of their obligations. I was glad I wasn't one of them. She patted an iron-colored curl back into place. "Some generous soul anonymously donated the funds we were trying to raise, so Bess and Patricia decided it wasn't in the town's best interest to bother with the lighting contest at all. Why waste our time, after all, when we already have the money?"

Since I'd recently come into money, a lot of it, actually, and since I had been the anonymous donor, I wasn't exactly certain what to say. It hadn't been my plan to derail the contest, only to take off the pressure of it needing to earn a certain amount of money. Until I found the body of Amber Hale during the one the previous year, I thought the event had been one of the most fun, and the rest of the attendees seemed to feel the same.

"I'm sorry, Martha, but I'm here, and I'm on board for going through with the contest if you are. What about Megan? Did she bail on us, too?"

As annoying as I found the woman, she hadn't been complicit in the whole Baxter Thomas ordeal, and I didn't think she'd killed Davina Benet, either. But since she'd popped up as a new arrival to town during the time in question, she sort of fit the profile, and so there were one or two questions I needed to ask her. Or maybe Martha would know the answers.

"Megan won't be helping with town functions anymore. She took a management position at a business in Bangor. A car dealership or an insurance agency. Something like that."

"That's a lousy drive to have to make every day. Worse in winter."

"I expect she'll move back down there before the end of the year."

"Move back?" I seized on the operative

phrase. "Is that where she's from originally?"

Martha squinted as she scanned her memory. "I think so. Or maybe it was Brewer. Not that it matters since those two towns are right next to each other, so it's almost the same thing. I was surprised when she said she wanted to go back, given the events that forced her to leave."

Intrigued, I cocked a brow at Martha. "What events?"

Eyes glittering with untold gossip, Martha gestured for me to sit, so I settled in to listen.

"This stays between you and me," she ordered but didn't bother to wait for me to agree, which I didn't, and as it turned out, I didn't need to. "What do you know about Chase Burke?"

The name rang a bell or two, or maybe

even a tower full of them.

"Plenty, and none of it good. He got in trouble for price-fixing, didn't he? Among several locally owned agricultural businesses. Busted after someone blew the whistle on him. He wasn't tied up with my ex-in-laws but was on their potential donors' watchlist because he did business with some of the foundation's contributors."

Martha tapped her nose.

"But how does Megan fit into the picture? The person who blew the whistle on him was high up in the company, right?"

Martha tapped her nose again, and this time, she nodded.

"It couldn't have been Megan, though. I'm sure I heard it was a man."

Eyes wide, Martha slowly shook her head.

"No," I argued. "It was. The news only

called him the 'trusted source' or something along those lines, but rumors were flying. It was a man, and there was a family connection. He was a cousin, maybe. Someone trusted because they were family." I rubbed my forehead to help pull out the memory. "Morgan. That's it. It was a man named Morgan Burke. I don't think I ever met him."

Her head tilted, Martha stared at me while she waited for the concept to penetrate.

"Oh, Morgan was Megan."

Martha nodded. "She wanted a fresh start, so she changed her name when she moved here. Morgan became Megan, and McCurdy was her mother's maiden name."

"I can see why she might feel the need." And that we'd had more in common than I'd known. No wonder she'd been so prickly all the time. I'd look into it in more depth. Still, if there had been any missing persons cases in that family, the information would have shown in the dossiers the foundation generated on the Burke family as potential donors. Based on what I could remember of those documents, I figured any connection between Megan/Morgan and Davina to be tenuous at best. So much for Megan's motive.

"Maybe I should have tried a new town and name as well."

"I'm glad you didn't. You've done so much for Mooselick River since you came home. For me, as well."

And there it was, because Martha had done plenty for me, too. I owed her whatever it took to put on a good event. "Then why don't we get settled in here and plan the best lighting contest in the history of ever?"

"Really, Everly. I don't see why we should bother," putting on a long-suffering air, Martha leaned back and fanned herself dramatically. "Lighting events are old-fashioned and a colossal waste of time."

That sounded like vintage Bess Tate.

"It's not a waste of time to bring wonder to the children and families of Mooselick River. It's not a waste of time to bring the community together. So what if we already have the money we need? We can have just as much fun with a free event. More, probably. Besides, we owe this to the town for putting up with extra traffic, tourists, and whatever else that's happened from the other events all year. We have to do the lighting contest, Martha. It's not even a question of should or should not. It's not a question of raising money but of raising spirits. Of raising community spirit, which will pay huge dividends in the long run. Now, are you with me?"

I hoped that raising spirits thing didn't turn out to be a literal event for me. The two I already had on my plate were more than enough. Still, my impromptu words stirred Martha's juices. Her eyes reflected something akin to fervor, and at that point, I realized I might have taken the speechifying a bit too far.

"We'll make it the biggest, best, most incredible lighting contest ever."

Since we'd only ever had one, I guessed that bar wasn't as high as she made it sound.

"Let's. I've got my sources on tap already,

and the press is cued up to start during the first week of December. We can use the same basic plan as last year unless you have something else in mind.”

Martha did.

“What if we added a snow sculpture contest to the roster of events?”

I paused and thought about the suggestion for a moment. “That could be fun, but since it depends on whether or not we have snow at all, and more, that we have the right type of snow, maybe we don’t advertise that aspect until closer to the event. We should leave some wiggle room to cancel if conditions are wrong.”

Nodding, Martha agreed, and then I brought up another important point.

“We also need to amend the rules to make sure we don’t have a repeat of what happened with Viola Montayne last year. This is an amateur contest, right? Everyone should have an equal chance, and I also think we should have both a business and a residential category."

Taking off the bifocal glasses she professed to hate, Martha set them aside. "I never thought we'd have enough businesses in town to qualify for a separate category. Do you understand what it means that we do?" Delicately, she wiped away a tear.

I reached across the table to pat her hand. "I do. It means all your years of planning have finally paid off."

"Maybe so, but you know I couldn't have done it without your help."

"Don't let me disturb the monthly meeting of the mutual admiration society."

Neither of us had heard Bess Tate walk through the front door. Probably by her design. Bess was a bit of a character and liked nothing more than to be where she shouldn't be and hear things no one wanted her to hear. She'd also had company from out of town during the week of the murder. Still, since she and her guests had inadvertently provided Patrea with an ironclad alibi, I figured there was no sense in asking potentially awkward questions.

"What are you doing here?" A blizzard would have felt like a warm day compared to the ice in Martha's tone. "I thought you didn't want to waste your time on something as fuddy-duddy as a Christmas lighting event."

Confirmed my earlier suspicion.

"Oh, come on now, you old cow. No way

I'm missing out on seeing Viola Montayne make a fool of herself, and I can't do that if we don't have something tailor-made to make it happen. Patty's right behind me. Had to make a potty stop."

"I should have known better than to ride with you. You're a menace to safe driving." Shooting me a smile, Patricia Croft took her customary place at the table. "If anyone's an old cow, it's you, Bess."

To diffuse whatever foolishness they had brewing between them, I detailed Martha's snow sculpture idea, and then Martha seemed to derive great joy in dismissing the meeting, which ticked Bess off, but then, most things did.

"You mean to tell me I hauled my old bones out in the cold for that?"

"Not my fault you showed up late, now, is

it?" Martha refused to take the bait. "Unless you have some great idea you want to share."

"It just so happens I do."

Martha waved her on. "The floor is yours."

As usual, all the tension centered around Bess while Patty sat and smiled, the type of smile that always made me wonder about her hidden depths. With all her bluster, Bess didn't hold anything back, but I thought Patty did, and if she ever truly got fired up, she'd go off like a volcano.

"I think we should add a second contest for all the local businesses to compete. Really jazz things up," Bess tilted her nose up just a bit as if to point out her superior thinking on the matter.

"You're a day late and a dollar short on that one," Martha practically crowed. "We've already added that to the slate for this season. Is there anything else?"

Bess deflated like a hot air balloon in an ice storm.

"Looks like you've thought of everything, then." She sulked until it was time to leave, then left in a huff when Patricia asked Martha for a ride home.

Before I left, I checked with Martha. If anyone could rattle off a list of recent transplants to town, it would be her.

"I know about Megan, Jason, and Nanette. Is there anyone else I've missed?"

"There's Leland Cobb and his pretty, new wife. She's named for one of the months. April, or May, I think. I only met her once."

Leland's name sparked a memory I couldn't pull completely clear, but since Martha had the info, I didn't have to.

"It's June," Patricia supplied. "Her name is June."

"Leland's Patricia's nephew, you know. Her brother isn't doing too well with his cancer treatments, so the kids decided to pull up stakes in Michigan and come back home. They sold their business there for a healthy profit, or so Patty says, and they've gone and bought the old mercantile building. For dirt cheap, I might add, because it needed a lot of work, but it's perfect for them because it has living space upstairs."

"That's the one with brown paper in the windows, right? A few doors down from Curated Collections? I've heard construction sounds from there."

Martha beamed. "We're getting a bakery around the first of the year."

"That's great news. When did they decide

to move back?" I'd only noticed the newspaper in the windows recently.

Patricia's smile held great fondness as she returned from a second trip to the lady's room. "We didn't tell my brother until the first of November when they rolled in with the moving truck, but they put their place up for sale in August, right after we got the bad news. Leland flew back to be here for that first chemotherapy session in September and then again for the closing in mid-October. We're praying for a miracle."

"I'll add your brother to my prayers as well, Patty. Is there anything I can do to help?"

She shook her head. "He has two more rounds of chemo, then two or three of radiation. It's helping to have Leland home, I think. I worry they won't make a go of the bakery, but I'm hopeful."

Okay, now, that was something I could help with. At least a little. Mentally, I laid out a plan to build some buzz around the new bakery, but the lack of proximity let out any overt connection from Leland to Davina's death.

"Speaking of," Martha held up a finger to indicate I should wait and left the old classroom to return moments later, holding a large basket wrapped in cellophane with a bow on top. "This is their welcome basket, and I haven't had a chance to drop it off. You could handle that for me, couldn't you?"

Since it gave me a chance to chat with the new couple and maybe poke around for any connection to Davina, I said I would be happy to deliver the basket, then got out of there before Martha came up with any other errands I could take off her hands.

CHAPTER FOURTEEN

"Come with me, now!"

Davina broke a rule by appearing in my bedroom. She broke another by talking to me before I'd had my first cup of coffee. I told her to buzz off and snuggled my back against Drew's.

"Get your lazy butt out of bed," she hissed. "Now! Your friend needs help."

"Which friend?" I wasn't even half awake yet, but I did get out of bed.

"The one across the street. Hurry up." The air snapped with the chill she gave off.

"There's no time for that," she added when I opened the dresser drawer for something to wear. To emphasize the point, she poked a hand through my chest.

"Don't do that. I'm moving as fast as I can." I slid my feet into a pair of fuzzy slippers, grabbed my bathrobe, and followed her out the door. Drew never even stirred, but Molly did. She let out a low growl as if she understood the danger and went to wait for me in the front hall.

"This way," Davina blew through the door while I grabbed a jacket against the cold, then poked her head back in. "Hurry up! There's no time to waste."

She had me worried. "What's wrong with Neena?" It was too early for the sun to do more than peek over the treetops and give off weak, watery light. The joys of autumn in

Maine. If Davina answered, I didn't catch what she said because my heart was pounding in my ears. "Never mind. Just tell me where she is."

Davina pointed toward Neena's house and zipped over there faster than my feet could take me.

Molly sped ahead, charged up the front steps, then dropped to her haunches and howled. I ran right out of my left slipper and left it in the driveway, forgotten. My bathrobe flared out behind me as I took the steps two at a time. The front door was locked, but I could hear Neena calling for help, so I didn't think twice.

"Get back, Molly." I grabbed the first thing I could find, a garden gnome, and broke the door glass pane nearest the knob. "I'm coming, Neena. Just hang on." Wrapping my bathrobe around my arm, I unlocked the door.

Molly ran past me in a flash, leaping over the broken glass and making her way inside. I didn't quite make it past the glittering shards unscathed and left smudges of blood on the floor without noticing the injury.

"Where are you?"

"Dining room," Neena yelled. "Help me, please. Hurry!"

I practically flew through the living room, dodged down the short hallway toward Neena's kitchen, and nearly skidded past the dining room beyond. A glimpse of the situation told enough of the story that I didn't need an explanation.

Her feet swinging from high above the floor, Neena dangled from what I hoped was a solidly anchored chandelier mounted to the vaulted ceiling. With the table pushed back, the area rug might have been thick enough to soften her fall, but Neena was too scared to chance the drop. Not with the stepladder she'd been using to replace the batteries in her smoke detector lying beneath her feet, making for a more treacherous landing.

"Hurry! My arms are shaking, and I'm losing my grip," she sounded hoarse, probably from shouting for help. "Thank God you heard me."

I righted the step ladder and positioned it so she could slide her feet onto one of the steps.

"You should be able to feel the ladder now. Go ahead and let go. One hand at a time," I ordered, then held the ladder steady while she transferred her weight to it. She let out a sigh of relief and just clung for a moment.

"I've got you." I reached up to give her some extra support while she gingerly made her way down. Neena simply sank to a seated position on the carpet when both her feet hit the floor. I wanted to go to her and offer a consoling hug, but I ignored the impulse. Instead, I went to the kitchen for a glass of water which she accepted gratefully.

"If you're okay, I'll get out of your way. Sorry I had to break a window to get in. Do you want me to send Drew over to seal it up for you?" Everything felt so awkward and broken between us that I figured I should leave.

"You're hurt," Neena noticed my one bare

foot and the bloody smudges.

"It's nothing." I turned my back on her and headed toward the door. "Sorry about the mess."

"Everly," Neena called out, and I stopped. "Thank you. If you hadn't heard me and come to my rescue, I'd have fallen."

Frustration sent a flush of prickly heat to my face. "But that's the thing, Neena. I didn't hear you." Turning back, I gave her a level look. "Davina did. She told me you needed help and practically forced me out of bed to come to your rescue, so I guess if anyone deserves your thanks, it's her."

With that as my parting line, I left Neena where she sat, and she didn't try to stop me. On the way home, Molly retrieved my lost slipper. With the ebbing of the adrenaline from my system, the pain from my cut foot had begun to set in. That was the reason for the tears slowly tracking down my cheeks.

Right.

Back home, I let Drew treat and bandage the cut, which he deemed wasn't deep or long enough for stitches after checking for remaining slivers of glass. Then I went down to the basement and beat the living daylights out of his heavy punching bag for a while. Half the time, I pictured Neena's face on the bag and the other half, Davina's.

Neither made me feel any better.

CHAPTER FIFTEEN

"Hey, I forgot to return your casserole dish." I didn't think to check if my mom was alone in her office, and I should have because she wasn't. "Oh, sorry, Jason. I didn't know you were here."

"I was just heading out, anyway." Jason's smile didn't reach his eyes, and I thought I detected hints of sadness in both. "Thanks for that recipe," he said to my mother. "And the conversation. I guess I have my answer."

When he'd gone, I noticed my mother's

expression was nearly as odd as Jason's. "What's up with him? Looked too intense to be about recipes."

My mother might not have explained or left her desk to hug me in the early days of my return home. We'd been on better terms since Davina shined a big old light on mom's psychic history and helped me better understand the roots of mine. When it comes to my mother, fewer secrets meant less angst. Who knew?

And for once, the secret-keeping had been on her side, not mine. Forgive me for feeling slightly smug.

"I wouldn't like to betray his confidence, but in this case, I think I will because it pertains to the mess you currently have on your plate. Jason's looking for his family. It's the reason he came to Mooselick River."

"Oh." Some of the puzzle pieces fell into place. "You think he's Davina's son?"

"Well," she said with gentle concern. "I know he's not mine, and now, so does he."

"Looks like I walked in on an awkward moment." One that had pivotal meaning for my murder investigation. "Did you tell him? About Davina maybe being his mother, I mean."

For Kitty Dupree, blushing was as rare as a lunar eclipse, but she did so now. "I should have, I'm sure. I couldn't find the words. He shouldn't hear that sort of news from a virtual stranger, don't you think?"

It was a hint, and not a gentle one because I could feel the weight of it bearing down on me as I took a seat across from her desk.

"You think I should be the one to tell him."

Not a question. A statement. "And that Davina should be present."

"Don't you?"

If she was right, and Davina was Jason's mother, he'd already missed his chance to get to know her. Still, I hesitated.

"What?" Mom asked. "Is there a problem? Surely, if there's a reason to break your rule about messages, this would be it."

But it wasn't the idea of outing myself as a seer of ghosts that bothered me. I'd become somewhat resigned to that type of thing. The real problem was that I hadn't fully ruled him out for her murder. I would, I supposed, have to dig into his alibi. One more time to make sure, and then, I'd have to face the other half of the issue: telling Davina.

"No," I said, "You're right. This would be the perfect reason to break the rules. Let me work out the best way to approach both of them with the possibility, okay? Then, you have my word. I will do what needs to be done."

She put her hand on mine. "You're a good girl. I know you'll do the right thing. Just don't put it off too long, okay?"

"I won't. I'll stop by the inn after I drop off the welcome basket for our newest enterprise. Did you know we're getting a bakery?"

"I did. Leland and June Cobb's place. I think it will be a welcome addition to our town, don't you?"

I grinned. "It doesn't suck."

"Nice language," my mother said, but without heat.

I gave her a peck on the cheek. "I'll get out of your hair, and don't worry, I'll be gentle with Jason."

Once I figured out if there was anything to be gentle about. Not that I had the first clue how to come up with definitive proof, but that was a problem for future me. Present me had errands.

When no one answered the front door of the old mercantile building, I went around to the back, where I could hear banging and sawing, and the door hung open.

"Knock, knock," I yelled. "Okay, to come in?"

"Up here," a voice wafted from a narrow staircase to my left, so I turned and began to mount.

"I've got a welcome basket for you." Jammed with stuff, wrapped in crinkly plastic, the thing barely fit up the stairs. I had to hold it up in front of my face, so I nearly tripped on the last step. A strong pair of hands grabbed my arm, righting me before I tumbled back down.

"Whoa, there. You okay?" The hands took the basket, leaving me to face our town's newest returning resident. "Leland. Leland Cobb, but everyone calls me Landy."

"Everly Dupree. I believe we went to school together." Finally, the nickname rang for me, and I remembered him. He'd filled out some, but the smile that split his round face was as wide as ever.

Smiling, Landy nodded. "We did. I remember you were a couple of years ahead of me. Let me get my wife." He set the welcome basket down. "She loves presents." He didn't so much get her as yell for her.

"I'll be there in a minute," June yelled

back.

"I work with your aunt Patricia on town projects sometimes. She's a lovely person. I'm sorry to hear about your dad's illness."

A shadow dimmed that smile, but only slightly. "Thank you. He's holding his own, and his oncologist seems optimistic, so we're getting through the treatments one day at a time."

"I'll keep him in my thoughts, and I'm sure he's happy to have you home."

"Who's this?" Landy's wife joined us, her smile nearly as bright as his. "I'm June." She offered a firm handshake.

"Everly Dupree. I brought you a welcome basket." I pointed to it. "And I was catching up with your husband. It's lovely to meet you."

Below a cap of platinum styled in an updo

that looked like white flame, June's face
held the same easy cheer as her husband's.

"Come on back. The place is a mess, still,
but we're making progress. I've got soft
drinks and a powerful need to rest my feet
for a minute."

Leland picked up the basket and handed it
back to me.

"I'll catch up with you later, Everly. If you
don't mind."

When I waved him off, he gave me
another grin and returned to whatever he'd
been doing while I followed his wife on a
quick tour of the living space that ended in a
tidy little kitchen where she pulled cans of
Coke from the fridge. I accepted mine,
waved off the need for a glass, and popped
the top.

"It's bigger up here than it looks."

"Right?" June looked around the open concept area with pride. "And it has that slightly industrial vibe to it. I feel like I'm living in a downtown loft or something. Not too bad considering how quickly this move came together."

"How are you liking it here so far?"

Again the quick grin on an openly mobile face. "Other than the accent being different, it feels a lot like home. Similar weather, though I understand you get more snow here, and people are the same wherever you go. Some are nice, some not so nice. Human nature always shows itself to the best advantage in the microcosm of small towns. Don't you think?"

"Sounds like you speak from experience."

June shrugged. "Guilty, and I wouldn't have it any other way but tell the truth. I've heard Mainers aren't very welcoming to outsiders. Should I be worried?"

My turn to shrug. "There are two types of outsiders. The first type comes for a visit, only to find they like the laid-back lifestyle enough to want to stay and adopt it for their own. Those people tend to fit right in."

June nodded. "Sure, that makes sense."

"Then there's the other kind. They come. They visit. They fall for the charm and decide to stay, but the charm wears thin before long. It begins to seem like a cover for being hopelessly behind the times. The next thing you know, they're getting involved in town business and trying to make things more like where they lived before. Progress is a good thing; we embrace it, but it sometimes moves slowly here."

Leaning back in her chair, June tilted her

head and gave me a long look, then another smile that made her eyes twinkle. "Human nature at its finest and most unknowable," she said. "Unless that was a warning."

"Not at all. My best advice is to keep an open mind and a sense of humor. This town is full of good people. A few odd ducks, but you'll have that. Like most anything, you'll get out of the experience what you put into it."

Saving me the awkwardness of bringing up the recent deaths, June leaned forward and lowered her voice. "Tell me the truth. What are the chances of being murdered in my bed? You've had a lot of trouble here in recent months."

My first instinct was to brush her fears aside, but I reconsidered.

"You're right." There was no sense in

denying the truth. "Two women are dead. The prevailing theory is they both died by the same hand and for personal reasons because these women were connected."

June nodded. "That's what Landy says, too. They were friends or something. He isn't worried, but he doesn't have to deal with my mother on the daily. I do. She's worried. Especially since we spent a night in that same room at the motel, it seemed like a safe place, but then this happened, and we learned it wasn't the first murder there. We slept in a murder motel."

A shudder ran through her. "We were at the hospital with my father-in-law the day she was killed and didn't know anything had happened until we passed the motel when we dropped my in-laws back home after the chemo."

Could I poke holes in the couple's alibi? Probably. The hospital wasn't that far away. Did I think they'd killed anyone? No, and there was no point in trying to make the circumstances fit when they didn't, but I still had to ask.

"Were you familiar with Davina Benet at all?"

"My mother watched her show. Bought into the myth, but I don't believe in all that psychic hokum."

I resisted the fleeting temptation to call on Davina and prove June wrong. Then, since she'd ruled herself and her husband out of my investigation, I changed the subject.

"Do you have a grand opening date set for the bakery? We've got a town-wide Christmas lighting contest planned. Last year's contest drew a crowd and generated some decent publicity." I gave her the details and was rewarded when she seemed delighted by the prospect.

"We were planning to open at the first of the year, but with a ready-made opportunity for publicity, we may be able to bump the date by a couple of weeks. Well, if we can find someone to help. Do you know anyone who might be looking for some extra work?"

"Give me your cell number. I'll check around and text you a list."

Because I had ideas for how to get their business off to a good start, we discussed advertising and branding for another fifteen minutes or so.

"I'll get out of your hair. You have plenty to do if you want to take advantage of the lighting event as a springboard to your grand opening. Call me if you need anything or have questions I can answer."

"You've made my day. Do you know that?" June's smile was as warm as the hand that landed on top of mine. "Thank you for the welcome basket and the much-needed push."

Even a month earlier, I'd have invited her to girl's night at Cappy's. Based on our brief conversation, I thought she'd slide right into our little group. But since I'd been slid out myself, that was no longer an option. Maybe later. If we patched things up.

"Anytime. Call me if you need anything. I really mean that. And welcome to Mooselick River. Despite the recent unpleasantness, it's a good place to live."

It would only get better once I solved Davina and Delilah's murders. On the way home, I contemplated the next step in that process and came up with an idea.

"Davina!"

She popped up in the passenger seat like a clown springing out of a wind-up box.

"What?"

"Did you keep photo albums? Ones going back to when you first began doing your work?"

We hit a bump, and her head went through the car roof. I'm not sure why I always found that type of thing amusing, but I did.

"Yes, why?"

I shrugged. "Just a hunch. I want to look at them if that's okay with you."

Her eyes went sad. "You're welcome to look at anything you want, but I don't need a trip down memory lane, so you're on your own."

"Fair enough."

Davina told me where to find what I wanted and faded out, leaving sadness behind like the Cheshire Cat's smile.

Since she'd likely be at home, cooking dinner, I called up Jacy's number and hit send. She answered quickly, but not without giving me a ration of grief.

"That case of friendship amnesia clear up, did it?" She didn't bother with hello.

"Looks that way. You have plans tonight?"

"Food, baby, husband. Not necessarily in that order, why?"

"I need to get back into Davina's house. Want to tag along?"

CHAPTER SIXTEEN

"I know she misses you," Jacy didn't even bother to keep her voice down. "Especially since you saved her from a broken leg, or worse."

"Shh," I said as I pulled out Davina's hide-a-key. "We're committing a major crime here. You could at least try to be quiet." Plus, I didn't want to talk about Neena.

"Pshaw," Jacy flicked her fingers at me. "We have permission from the owner, and there's no one around. I don't think Ernie's been here since the last time we were."

"Getting permission from a ghost probably wouldn't impress Ernie, and I'm pretty sure it wouldn't hold up in court."

"It might if she showed herself," but Jacy lowered her voice slightly, which was all I wanted. "What are we looking for again?"

I shrugged. "Photo albums. Davina said she kept some from the early years and told me where to look for them. You didn't have to come. It shouldn't take me more than a few minutes, but I'm glad you did."

Grinning, she pointed to her black watch cap. "And let you push me away again, only to miss out on another chance to snoop around? I don't think so." Jacy moved toward the door as I replaced the key in the box and stashed it back in the bird feeder where Davina had kept it hidden. "I only wish you'd given me enough notice to paint

266

my nails properly. This pink just doesn't scream sneaky."

"I wasn't pushing you away." My attempt to defend myself came off weak because I could see how Jacy would feel the way she did. "But I will admit this is more fun with my partner in crime."

"Everything is." Jacy grinned again.

The house had begun to take on the stale odor of disuse. "Smells kind of funky in here," I said. "Like mine did that first day. Kind of musty-dusty. Empty. It's a shame."

"Did you know Davina bought this place fifteen years ago? She'd been planning to move back for quite a while. From what I hear, it's going on the market as soon as Ernie gives the okay so Tim can clear everything out. If it had been on the market when I bought mine, I'd have been tempted to put in an offer."

"It's a nice property. Lots of space for a growing family." I offered a broad hint.

"Nothing doing on the baby front, but we're still trying."

"That's the fun part."

Not that I would know from experience. Paul hadn't thought we were ready for children, and Drew was the old-fashioned type who wanted them but not without being married first. Still, I was closer to saying yes than I ever had been. Maybe, once I'd sent Davina along on her merry way, and didn't have a lifetime of being haunted ahead of me, Drew and I could start planning a family.

"It's not quite as fun when there's so much pressure on the act, but we're making it work."

"You could sell your place and buy this one. I know for a fact it won't be haunted."

"Tempting." Jacy got to the office ahead of me and pulled down the shade at the single window above Davina's desk. "Where'd she say to look?"

Gently, I moved past her, headed toward the far wall and the built-in bookshelves and cabinets where Davina kept her photo albums. "Should be in one of these cabinets. You start at that end. I'll start on this one. We'll meet in the middle."

Except we didn't get that far because I found the albums and a series of what looked like high-end scrapbooks in the second cabinet I opened.

"Got them," I pulled out one of the scrapbooks and flipped the cover. "And a bonus besides. There are several books of press clippings put together by one of those services. It's not the one Paul's family used to use for the foundation, though. This company did a much better job on the binding." Raised by a master bookbinder, I had developed an eye for that type of thing.

"They have services for that?" Jacy grabbed the book away from me. "We should get them to do one for you."

Behind her back, I rolled my eyes. "Sure, because having a visual record of the events leading up to and after my divorce would be aces."

"I meant for stuff you've done here. You've had a lot of good press, too, you know."

"Martha would love it if we had one done to chronicle the town, though. I guess there's been talk of setting up a historical society or something. Maybe I'll look into it on her behalf."

Jacy joined me, took some of the albums as I removed them from shelves, and handed them back to her. "I don't think taking them home is a good idea. That would be evidence tampering."

"Like this isn't?" The tiny penlight clamped between Jacy's teeth shined in my eye, nearly blinding me.

I blinked and held up a hand to shield my tender orbs. "The way I see it, there are degrees of tampering."

There weren't, and I knew that well enough but decided I didn't care about a tiny bit of law-breaking. My intentions were in the right place, and the fluttering in my gut said we were onto something.

"We need more light."

"Hall closet?" From our last breaking and

entering experience, we knew the closet was light-safe at least. "It'll be a tight fit, but I don't feel right about removing anything from the house."

"Then, we won't. You take those, I'll get these, and we'll see what we see. Anything good, we use our phones to take pictures like they used to do with those tiny spy cameras in movies."

Scanning through the clippings turned up exactly nothing we hadn't already seen online, so we sat together, our backs against the pile of boxes, and paged our way through Davina's life in photographs.

"Look, that's our moms. They looked so young there." Jacy pulled out her phone and lined it up to take a photo of the photo. "So happy." She checked the quality of the image on her phone and took another.

"Does it have a date? It must have been taken before the Ouija board incident."

"You look like your mom. Like in the face, just not the hair," Jacy gently pulled the photo from the album for a closer look.

"There was a time that comment would have put you on my list, but Kitty and I are in a good place these days, so I'll consider that a compliment." I took the photo and held it under the light. "You and Momma Wade have the same smile, but you have your daddy's eyes."

Jacy nodded. "I do. I'm sending you a copy of this." Fingers flying, Jacy texted the better of the two photos, then got back to the job at hand. "I know she gave us permission to be here, but it feels like we're spying on Davina's life. She should have come with us, so we know what we're looking at."

"Ghosts are less helpful than you want them to be. I think it's like a rule or something. She knew we were coming, but she doesn't like being here when the house practically echoes with emptiness."

"I'm done with this one. Let's call it Davina: The High School Years. I didn't see anyone staring at her with unrequited longing or anything, so I'm calling it a bust. Moving on." Jacy chose another album while I continued to leaf through mine.

"Nothing in this one, either. Looks like travel shots mostly." I put it down and selected another. "This one looks promising," I said when several shots on the third page matched up with a photo from one of the news clippings of her first case. "She told me about finding that little girl and how the uncle who kidnapped her said he only wanted to take care of her."

I flipped to the next page, then, less gently than I should have, I shoved the album under Jacy's nose. "That one wasn't in the news reports, and I can see why."

Sorrow rode Jacy's features and probably my own as well. Taken at the pivotal moment when the police officer was passing the child back to her father, the little girl leaned away from him as hard as she could, her arms reaching for the man in handcuffs.

"Look at his face, though." Jacy flicked on the flashlight app on her phone, juggling it and the penlight so we could see even better. "The uncle, I mean. He's not even concerned that he's being arrested. He's just looking at her like she was his prized possession being taken away. It gives me the creeps."

I pulled out my phone and snapped a copy of that one for myself and a few others before putting the album back in the pile.

"Here's a nice one," Jacy passed her album over and pointed to a shot of Davina on a boat with her brother, Tim. "Look how happy she is with the wind in her hair and that huge smile. It makes me feel better to know she had more than just sad stories in her life. Her work must have taken a toll."

"Quite a toll, I'd say. She can't be more than thirty in this one, and she's going gray. The picture's dated, and she was only a year or two older than our mothers, so that's math I can do in my head."

"I wonder if that's why she went blond," Jacy speculated. "Some people do because it's easier to hide gray roots."

I nudged Jacy's shoulder with mine. "I know. Do you remember when Grammie Dupree did that home dye job right before my cousin's wedding? She wanted to get rid of the gray but went way too dark and dyed her scalp the color of ink?"

"I do. She was quite a woman. I miss her." Jacy had run tame in my house since we'd met in Kindergarten, and in the spirit of the more, the merrier, Grammie Dupree treated her like she'd been born there. "I miss her a lot."

"Me, too." I got misty. Of all the dead people in my life, my grandmother would be the one I'd have welcomed back as a ghost. According to the medium who assessed my haunting situation, that wasn't possible. But then again, Kat hadn't known about my mother, so it might be time for another visit because some of the things she'd told me weren't adding up.

Then Jacy dropped a bomb. "Tim dyes his hair, too."

"Really? I never noticed." But now, I was picturing him in my head.

Jacy shrugged. "He doesn't know I know about it, but he goes to a salon in Bangor. It's near the place where they did my fertility testing. I happened to catch a glimpse of him through the window, but I don't think he saw me, and I figured if he went to that much trouble, he didn't want anyone to know."

"You're a good woman, Jacy Dean."

"I have my moments."

When I flipped the album closed, a loose photo fell out. Jacy grabbed it before I could.

"Ooh." She took a look, then waved it at

me, "Hot guy on a bike. Do you think he's the one she did the wild thing with? This could be the missing baby daddy."

I snatched the photo from her and took a closer look. Was it my imagination, or did the boy's eyes look familiar? And the shape of his mouth.

"Gah. You know what all this means, don't you?" I set aside the albums, raised my knees, and used them to prop up my elbows so I could drop my head in my hands.

"No, what?" I felt Jacy's hand on my arm. "Is it bad?" she asked.

"A while back, Jason approached my mother to ask if she was his mother."

"Get out!" It had been too long since Jacy and I talked. She was behind on a lot of the news. "You think he's Davina's baby that she gave up?"

"He tracked his birth mother to Mooselick River. I'm not sure how because I haven't wanted to ask the awkward questions, but I did look at Jason's employment application, and I can tell you he's several years younger than he looks."

Jacy frowned as it took her a moment to process, then she pointed to the photo album. "Prematurely gray hair could be an inherited trait if both Davina and Tim have it. Which means if Jason went gray early, he could be Davina's son."

"That and he has his father's eyes." I snatched up the photo again, grabbed my phone, and made a copy while Jacy studied the shot without getting in my way.

"You're right."

"It has to be. I mean, it makes sense. It's nothing you could even remotely consider as proof, but it adds enough weight I'll have to broach the subject with him. Her, too. Just hand me an opener, would you? I have this lovely can of worms that needs tossing everywhere."

Catching on quickly is one of Jacy's gifts. "You don't think it's enough to tell him who his mother was? You think you'll need to get them together if you can, which means you'll have to tell him your truth."

"In a nutshell, but there's more. He's been on my list of possible murder suspects, but I won't have a choice if his alibi holds. I'll have to out myself and give them their moment. It's too bad Davina didn't have DNA test results in her little safe. That would make my life a lot easier."

"If Jason's not grateful for what you're trying to give him, I'll personally volunteer to toss a bucket of water on his head.”

“Thanks, I think.” Reaching over, I gave Jacy’s hand a squeeze.

Squeezing back, she said, “Are we done? It’s getting stuffy in here.”

With difficulty, I heaved myself up off the floor, reached down to give Jacy a hand up. “I guess we are. A wasted effort on the murder front, but at least we got to spend time together. I’ve missed this.”

"Just remember, that was by your own choice.”

I reached up, flicked the light off, and sighed. “I know.”

The sentimental moment passed. We put everything back where we’d found it and kept to the shadows at the side of the road as we made our way to the turn-around where I’d parked. Still, we kept to less awkward subjects on the ride back to Jacy's house, and I went in for just a few minutes because, with darkness coming so early, we were there in time to put little Wade to bed.

With his mother's sweet disposition and his father's unflagging energy, Wade was a handful and cute as a button. Because he was hard to resist, I ended up reading him three bedtime stories before kissing him goodnight. Jacy had a future heartbreaker on her hands.

I had a conundrum on mine. How much to tell, and to whom, and when.

CHAPTER SEVENTEEN

On my way to the inn, I stopped in at the grocery store and wrestled a giant bag of dog food onto the conveyor belt because Robin Thackery couldn't handle the scanning wand and everyone knew it.

"I'm on team Everly," Robin leaned forward, kept her voice conspiratorially low, and made a weird, three-fingered gesture.

"Okay, thanks." I had no idea what she was talking about, but with Robin, it was almost always best to remain ignorant.

"No, I mean it. I'm on your side."

Okay, I had to. "My side of what, exactly?"

"You know." Gum snapped between Robin's teeth as she cocked her head to look at me and failed to scan the next two items but scanned the third twice. I probably should have just gone to the service desk, to begin with, since I ended up there nearly every time I had the misfortune to get in Robin's line. She made the three-fingered gesture a second time.

"If I knew, I doubt I'd be asking."

Robin shrugged. "How am I supposed to know what you don't know?"

A deep, cleansing breath later, I said, "What's team Everly?"

"I mean, if you can't trust one of your best friends, who can you trust? Am I right? I mean, really. Almost the same thing happened to me once. I called dibs on the last tube of Scarlet Harlot lipstick, and then my best friend just grabs it right out from under me."

Hello, tangent. Robin will be your rider today.

I spent the next few seconds trying to figure out the last time I'd bought a new lipstick and decided a trip to Sephora might be in order, but I still couldn't see any correlation to Robin's babbling.

"Real shame." I resorted to the old nod-and-smile routine.

"I mean, she's pretty and all, and you know, since her husband died, she probably hadn't gotten her boomchickawow on in a while, but that's no excuse for snaking your man even if he owns that inn now. That doesn't make him so much of a catch. You'll find someone better."

Halfway through the act of pulling out my wallet, a couple of things tripped.

"Are you talking about Neena Montayne and David Barrington?"

Robin nodded. "Dirty, man-stealing traitor and the jerk who couldn't resist her."

A band of tension settled around my forehead. "Neena and David are seeing each other?"

"That's what I heard, and word on the street is you and her had a rift."

Robin wasn't wrong about the rift, but I'd hoped David and Neena would get together, so other than the fact that there seemed to be some sort of division with teams involved, I was happy for them. Neena might not want anything to do with me, but I still cared enough to wish her the best.

"And there are teams? What are the teams

for? I don't understand." That is pretty much the baseline when dealing with Robin.

"You know Carlene Nicholson?" I heard the person in line behind me let out a long-suffering sigh, and I chose to be rude. He could wait a minute until I got to the bottom of whatever was going on. If it involved Carlene Nicholson, it couldn't be good.

"She's back? I thought she moved away."

Robin shrugged. "Maybe. She's back now, and team Neena all the way."

Given a choice between the devil and me, Carlene would ink the deal for her soul without batting an eyelash.

"She's what you might call the captain of team Neena."

Again, no surprise to me. "Was all this team stuff her idea?"

Behind me, the next guy in line cleared his

throat impatiently. I knew it wasn't nice, but I flicked my fingers at him without turning around.

"Maybe. I don't know. Some people were betting on you and him getting together." The last of my groceries went into a bag. I'd lost track of how many mistakes she'd made and decided to call it even.

"Tell Carlene and whoever else is on these ridiculous teams that David and I have never been an item and never will be. We're not interested in each other. Not romantically, at least. Our parents are friends, and he's more like a brother to me than anything else."

Robin threw me a skeptical brow lift. She looked confused, but no more so than usual, I guessed.

"He was at your house for Thanksgiving,

wasn't he?"

What did that have to do with anything?

"Yes, but as friends. I have a boyfriend who was also at my house for Thanksgiving since he lives there. I'm with Drew. People must know I'm with Drew."

Didn't they? We'd been seen together in public enough that our relationship couldn't be that well-kept of a secret. Cappy's was the place to see and be seen, and we'd done dinner and dancing there countless times. What was wrong with people?

Except I wasn't talking to *people*, I was talking to Robin, who got most of her daily exercise from jumping to wrong conclusions. A pursuit she'd honed to a fine art.

"Who's Drew?" Robin frowned.

"Drew. Andrew Parker. Owns the fitness center." Every word I uttered fell on the stony silence of Robin's frown of incomprehension. "Drew."

A cart gently nudged me in the back, and I whirled to give its user a piece of my mind.

"What the—" The tirade I planned to dump on the jerk behind me died in my throat when I found myself staring at my man. In the flesh—eyes dancing with laughter, he'd listened to the entire conversation. I pointed to him and said, "That's Drew. We're together."

"Okay," Robin said in that tone people use when talking to the very young or the very old—or someone they think might be suffering from hallucinations. I was none of those things, and Drew was as real as real gets, but you couldn't prove that by the way Robin acted. And really, what do you do in these situations?

I shook my head and left. Several minutes later, Drew strolled out of the store and joined me.

"That was surreal." Good humor still lit his handsome features as he leaned down to take my lips in the sweetest of kisses.

"That was Robin," I corrected gently. "Surreal is her middle name, I think. But that does explain why people have been making that weird gesture at me the past few days. I think it's meant to be an E to show they're on team Everly."

"You know I'm always on team Everly," Drew's voice tickled my cheek.

"I do, and you know David and I are just friends…family, really."

"I do," he said in a tone that made me think of vows and happily ever afters. Scary stuff, but maybe not so much as before. "I also know how much you miss having Neena in your life, but it will all work out in the end."

"I hope so."

Ten minutes later, David stared at me as if I'd grown a second head. "People thought we," he pointed to me, then jammed his thumb into his chest, "were a couple?"

From behind me, I heard a snort. I turned to see Miranda from Cappy's holding a spray bottle and a rag.

"I didn't know you worked here," I said. David had mentioned hiring, but I didn't expect him to move so quickly.

"Temp job." Miranda said. "Nanette had something come up. She asked me to fill in. I needed the money, so here I am, but enough about me. What's this about you and David being a couple?"

"That's the current theory." I turned to David. "You don't have to look horrified. You'd be lucky to have me."

"Right back at you."

Now that we had established we were both a catch, I asked the question I'd come to ask.

"Do you remember the day Davina died?"

He managed to frown and look surprised at the same time. "Yeah, why?"

"Jason worked that day, right?"

Taking a moment to cement his thoughts, David nodded. "He did, but only because we had a problem with one of the ovens, and he wanted to be here when the repairman came. The guy showed up two hours late, and then it only took him fifteen minutes to fix the problem. Why do you want to know?"

"It's nothing." I shook my head. "Just

following up on an idea I had. You're certain he was here the entire time?"

"You could set your watch by his pacing from the kitchen to reception to see if the guy had arrived."

Okay, one person off the murder list, and another chore added to my ongoing one.

Getting Jason and Davina together seemed inevitable. If only I had definitive proof they were related, I wouldn't worry so much about doing the wrong thing.

CHAPTER EIGHTEEN

"Hey, that's Davina on TV. Where's the remote?"

We'd turned the volume down to discuss our plans for the weekend. Drew wanted to do something outdoorsy, like a long hike, and I wanted to drive to Portland to see a contemporary photography exhibit at the art museum. Halfway through discussing a side trip to Cape Elizabeth to see the famous Portland Head Light lighthouse as a compromise, Davina's face on the screen caught my attention.

"I found it," Drew pointed the remote at the TV, cranked the sound way up, cringed, and tapped it down a couple of notches. "Missed most of the story. Let me back it up."

"The loss of J. Baden Pingree follows mere weeks after the tragic death of Davina Benet, who played an instrumental role in the highly publicized kidnapping of his only daughter, poor little Nancy Pingree," the reporter let her voice dip into pathos at the end.

Photos of the family and newspaper clippings flashed across the screen while the reporter gave a brief rundown of the case, followed by a few snippets of information I already knew about the family history. The reporter painted the uncle/kidnapper as a monster, nearly gloating about his subsequent death in prison. The story ended with an oblique reference to Davina possibly being named in Pingree's will.

"I guess we'll never know for sure, but did you notice who was missing from all of that?" I grabbed the remote and reversed to the beginning to watch the whole thing again.

"Lots of information about the circumstances of the kidnapping, but not much about the little girl, and nothing at all about her now."

"Bingo," I sang out. "I saw a photo of poor little Nancy in an album at Davina's. She didn't look nearly as happy to be found as that reporter made it seem. And wouldn't you think they'd have at least mentioned her in the context of her father's death?"

Drew reversed the report a third time and

ran it through slowly, pausing to look at the press clippings as they scrolled past. "You know what else is missing here? Where was the mother then? I didn't see her in any of the photos or any of the text that's readable. And where is she now?"

"She was mentioned in the articles I read, but only peripherally. Too devastated to speak to the press. Heavily sedated and sequestered for her mental health. That type of thing. The story mostly centered around the tragic figure of the grieving father willing to try anything to get his daughter back and the shiftless uncle who saw dollar signs when he looked at his niece."

"That's some cold-hearted BS right there. How much did he think she was worth?"

I shrugged. "It didn't get that far, I guess.

Davina led the police to the girl before the uncle had a chance to deliver the ransom demand. There was some speculation about that in the press. Most kidnappings for ransom move at a different pace since the money is the main consideration. The police put it down to the snatch and grab being a spur-of-the-moment thing."

Drew let the report play at regular speed and watched the video clip of J. Baden Pingree speaking passionately to the camera begging for the return of his precious child.

"I can only imagine how that must have felt. Worst thing for a parent to experience."

I nodded because the truth of the comment shivered along my spine. "Paul grew up under the possibility of something like that happening. I'm not saying that's what twisted him into the moron he turned out to be, but I can't imagine adding that worry to all the rest of the ones that come with being a parent."

"I'd like two," Drew changed the subject. "One of each would be nice, but I'm not picky. If you had a different number in mind, I'm okay with that, too."

"You're getting a little ahead of yourself, don't you think?"

But Drew shook his head. "Not at all. I've seen your face when Wade gives you kisses. You want babies, and I want to be the one to give them to you. I'm not going anywhere, and I'm not Paul. When the time is right, we will make a family."

"And what if one of our kids ends up like

me?"

"What? Beautiful inside and out? Willing to leap into the fray to protect and help someone she didn't know well? With wild, glorious red hair, freckles, and a tendency to blush? What a tragedy that would be."

I didn't just appreciate his sarcasm. I loved him even more for it.

"I meant haunted, and you know it."

"Haunted, special, wonderful. It's all the same to me, all part of the Everly package. Nothing bad in handing that down to the next generation. I love you. I'll love you with ghosts, without ghosts; the same goes for our babies."

There wasn't much to say in the face of such confidence, so I told him I loved him, kissed him, and pretended I wasn't thinking about wedding dresses for the rest of the evening.

While getting ready for bed, my thoughts cycled back to the news report, and I realized they hadn't mentioned the cause of J. Baden Pingree's death. Weird.

CHAPTER NINETEEN

After Drew left for work the next morning, I quickly searched, only to learn that the cause of Pingree's death hadn't been reported. While I had my laptop open, I downloaded the photos from my phone, printed them out, and sorted them into two piles. One contained images that had more to do with her personally, and the other included those that belonged on Patrea's murder board.

An hour later, I pinned the photos in place while Patrea and Delilah watched.

"I know that face," Delilah leaned closer to the board. Close enough that when she swayed, her nose went right through it. "I've seen that face recently." She pointed to the photo of the little girl from Davina's first case.

"She'd be all grown up now." Patrea and I shared a sidelong glance that fairly dripped skepticism.

"Really?" Delilah's response held an equal level of sarcasm. "Thanks for the news bulletin. However, did I survive all these years without you around to tell me every little thing?"

In a moment of perfect synchrony, Patrea and I both tilted our heads and looked at her. If ghosts could blush, Delilah would have when our unspoken point hit her.

"I get it. I'm dead. Ergo, I didn't survive. I

don't understand why you think I can't possibly be useful. Except, I'm right, but I can't think whose face it is. It's too bad we don't have my cell phone because I have an app that does age progression on photographs."

"Really? What's it called?" My phone was in my pocket. "I'll download it right now."

She told me, and I did. We crowded around the tiny screen, Delilah giving me a solid dose of the creepy crawly chills while I cued up the app and selected the little girl's photo. We got the spinning screen of death for a solid minute before a message popped up saying the image wasn't clear enough to use.

"Great idea in theory, just didn't pan out in practice," Patrea said. "Can you do anything to clear up some of these pixels? Maybe try one of the sharpening filters?”

“I know what those words mean individually, but if you put them together, it turns to gibberish.”

“I’ve got it,” Patrea pulled out her phone and opened the one we needed since she’d already had me send her the photos. “Most phone cameras have built-in filters, let’s run through a few options, and if that doesn’t work, I’ll look for a better app.”

I watched over her shoulder as she tapped the edit button, and a new screen popped up. “This one,” she pointed to the enhance button, “is a one-stop deal.” She tapped the button, and the image instantly looked brighter and clearer.

“I did not know you could do that.”

“Oh, I’m just getting started.” The other thing about Patrea is once she sets her feet on a path, she doesn't give up. She slid the first set of buttons aside until she found one marked: Adjust.

"I didn't know you could do that, either."

"Now," Buttons whizzed past as Patrea flicked the screen to find the one that would sharpen the image, "we'll see what's what." She adjusted the slider by tiny increments until the girl's face was as clear as it would get. "Best I can do."

The wheel spun for less time but gave the same message.

"What next?" I said. "We could go back to Davina's and steal the original, but I can tell you it doesn't look as good as this."

"No," Patrea said. "I have a better idea. These phone apps are fine, but I have professional-grade editing software on my office computer, and while I'm no wizard at using it, I know enough to make it work for this. What do you think?"

"I think we need to move on and get this done while I have enough juice to stay visible," Delilah answered before I could.

"How long will that be, exactly?" Careful not to come in contact with Delilah, Patrea circled her and went back to the board to look at the copy of the photo pinned there.

"My office computer is a workhorse, but it's not all that speedy. Old newsprint tends to be grainy, so I think it could take a while to process. I can't say exactly how long."

"It might be best if you conserve your energy, Delilah. Meet us at the office in an hour or so," I suggested.

"You're trying to get rid of me because you know time doesn't work the same way over here."

Delilah was only half right. I'd just as soon not have her hovering in Patrea's tiny office while we worked, but this was the first I'd heard of the time thing.

"I didn't know time was fluid on your side," I admitted. "But if you stay within hearing distance, I'll call you before we run the photo through the app again."

Patrea nodded. "Would it help if I also give my word we won't move forward without you?"

Apparently, it would. "You'd do that for me?" Delilah looked ready to cry with her hand going to her heart, which I assumed was a remembered gesture. Her shocked surprise made me wonder if she'd suffered in love or chased after Davina because she hadn't made other friends. Sad either way.

"Of course." I followed Patrea toward the

front hall, where our coats hung from the newel post. Once she got an idea in her head, Patrea was the type to follow through without delay. Admirable, yet also annoying at times. "We'll zip over and get things set up."

"Okay. Don't forget, though."

"This was your idea. We won't forget."

We parted ways at the door, and since my car was behind hers, Patrea piled in, then fell into an odd silence. When we pulled up in front of her office, I turned to her and didn't shut off the engine right away.

"Are you okay with all of this?" I put my hand on her forearm and gave it a squeeze. "I know the missing persons part of this case hits close to home, and if it's too much, I'm sure I could scare up someone to fix that photo for me."

"No. I want to. Aging software probably won't help us find Justin, but if I run his photo through, I will have a better idea of what my brother would look like today. It doesn't sound like much, but it helps. If Davina was right, and with her track record, I'd like to think she was, he's living his life somewhere. Looking like those computer-generated photos somewhere. That will be much more than I had before, and because it will, I need to familiarize myself with the process. I need to do this."

"Okay. Then, we will."

Resolute, I switched off the engine and followed her inside.

It only took twenty minutes to clean up the photo, and I spent part of that time looking for a better app.

"Hey," I flipped my phone to show Patrea

the search results list. "Did you know they have a baby app, too?" When she frowned, I elaborated. "If I put in my photo and Drew's, it will meld our features and estimate what our baby would look like."

"I don't know if that's cool or creepy."

"A little of both, I think. What if you put the results of that one into the age progression app? Then you'd get to see your baby grow up."

"Nope. That's definitely seven steps over the creepy edge."

I shrugged. "Maybe." But I was tempted and might have tried it if my inbox hadn't dinged with the results of Patrea's efforts.

"Delilah!"

She showed up so fast I figured she'd been hanging around outside or something. "I'm here."

"Here we go." I uploaded the photo, and we all watched the circle spin. This time, when it stopped, a slider appeared. Breathless anticipation made my finger shake just a little as I touched the screen and began to swipe slowly right.

"Oh. My. God." Delilah echoed my thoughts when the child's face thinned and lengthened. Slowly, the face morphed into someone we all recognized.

"That's Nanette Hill," I said as several clues floating around in my head clicked into place. "Nanette…Nancy. That's really close, and she wears gloves when she's working, and that cleanser she uses smells like carnations. I should have seen it before."

"Call Ernie," Patrea said. "Let him handle this. You've just healed up from your last foray into solving crime."

"He can't right now because she's out of town," I said, shaking my head. "Now that we know who she is, I figure she's gone to her father's funeral. Probably stuck around for the reading of the will. Listen, I know where David keeps the master key. Before I talk to Ernie, I want to search her room for proof."

Patrea disagreed, and we argued all the way back to the flip house and then for a bit longer until I let her think she'd won without having to make any promises. A fine line that Patrea wouldn't appreciate, but I wouldn't sleep until I got my snoop on.

I didn't notice Neena's car parked behind the inn because I chose a spot where Patrea couldn't look out her window and see mine, but my former friend sat behind the desk when I went in. One look at her and I nearly turned around and left, but this was getting past the point of ridiculous, so my stubborn streak kicked in, and I didn't.

"David around?" Best to tell him what we'd found and get permission to search Nanette's room if I could.

Neena shook her head. "He went to Bangor. With Nanette out of town, and no guests, he gave Jason the day off, so I'm here alone, watching the phone. As a favor."

"Okay. Thanks." I turned to leave. Better to come back later than deal with her on top of Nanette. Except it wasn't because I didn't know when Nanette would return, and time was of the essence. "If you don't mind, I need to check something. You stay here. I'll be in and out as quickly as possible."

While my words were passably polite, my tone carried an edge to it that made Neena flinch. I probably should have been more concerned for her feelings, but pissed off nudged concern out of the way, and took over my mood.

Without looking in her direction, I bypassed the front desk and stepped into the office. I should have known she'd follow me as I opened the drawer and grabbed the master key. Since my brain refused to provide words I might not regret later, I said nothing.

I figured I'd handled it wrong when she followed me toward the stairs. Or that there hadn't been a right way.

"I'm fine. You don't have to come."

No answer, but her footsteps echoed mine down the hallway to Nanette's private quarters. It took some oomph, but I pretended Neena was a puff of smoke—

ugly, oily smoke—and imagined her wafting toward the ceiling while I began my search in the living room.

I didn't know exactly what I was looking for, but I didn't find anything incriminating there or in the bathroom, and I even checked inside and behind the toilet tank. However, I hit it big in the bedroom with Nanette's bottom dresser drawer.

"Dirty, rotten killer," I muttered as I carefully moved aside a stack of old sweaters and uncovered Delilah's missing purse and phone, along with an empty gun safe just big enough for a small pistol or maybe a revolver. "I knew it was you."

"Nanette killed someone?"

"Davina Benet, and Delilah Cannon."

If Neena hadn't been leaning against the door frame watching me, we'd have both been sunk because she was the only one who heard the side door open and close on the floor below.

Busted.

"It's too early for David or Jason to be back, so that has to be Nanette," Neena hissed. "We need to get out of here."

We might not have been friends anymore, but we agreed on that.

"I'm right behind you." I debated grabbing the purse, but there wasn't time, so I hastily shoved the drawer closed. "Go." I practically pushed Neena toward the door leading to the rear stairs. It didn't help that the door stuck when she yanked on the knob, then freed itself to slam against the wall.

"Who's there?" Nanette called out. "Everly? Is that you?" She must have looked out the window to see my car. "Have you been going through my things?"

Neena let out a low-pitched squeal, but at least I didn't need to tell her to be quiet as we closed the door behind us and climbed.

CHAPTER TWENTY

"Why don't you call for help?" Her breath coming faster, Neena's eyes were glassy with fear.

"Left my phone in the car. Where's yours?"

She shook her head. "Front desk."

"It's fine," I said. "I have a plan."

What I had was more of a wish, but Neena didn't need to know I was banking on calling on one of the ghosts once we got to a relatively safe location. Davina could alert Leandra. Leandra could call Ernie. Ernie could do his job and come to our rescue, meaning I might not end up strangled, beaten to death, or shot. In the meantime, we needed to hide, and I had just the place. I went up another flight of stairs, motioning for Neena to come along.

"Why the hell are we going up? Haven't you ever watched a horror movie before? People go up, next thing you know, they're on the roof and then the ground, and then, they die. I don't want to fall or get pushed off the roof. I don't want to die."

"Follow me, and keep quiet." Careful to let the thick carpeting muffle our footsteps, I practically dragged Neena deeper into the private section of the building. "We're not going to the roof, but I know a place where we'll be safe until help comes."

Between the ghost of the former resident, a man I'd already sent into the light, and the current owner who'd asked for my help with remodeling, I knew every single one of the inn's darkest secrets. As a child, Delly Barker had loosened one of the panels at the end of the hall near his bedroom so he could slip into the crawlspace behind. He'd told me about it once while I'd helped him make his way properly into the afterlife. If I could get us there before Nanette made it to this area of the inn, it would buy time to figure out our next move.

Downstairs, in the public areas, Nanette searched for us, calling our names in tones that alternated between wheedling and commanding.

"Get in." I counted over and shoved the top of the third panel, so the bottom flipped up and out. "Quickly but quietly, and don't worry, the space behind here is bigger than it looks. Go straight back. Keep your head down. I'll be right behind you."

Cringing against possible spiders and dust, Neena did as I said. I didn't waste a second following her into the crawlspace. She let out a squeak as I pulled the panel shut and cut off what meager light it had allowed.

In the pitch black, we settled with our backs against the rough wood, letting our breathing return to as normal a pace as it could given that a madwoman was in the building and she'd killed at least twice already.

"I'll call Davina and send her to get help. It could take a while, so we'll have to wait." I don't know which of us I was trying to reassure. "We just have to stay quiet and wait it out." I closed my eyes and willed my shoulders to relax before the tension brought on a migraine.

"I'm scared," Neena's voice whispered through the darkness.

As much as I wanted to touch her, hold her hand, offer physical comfort, she'd proved she didn't want any of that from me. "You'll be safe here," I whispered back. "I don't think Nanette knows there's a crawlspace behind the wall."

"I'm not scared of Nanette, you idiot."

"Great." I bent my legs and wrapped my arms around them to give her access to the exit. "Well, there's the panel. Go ahead and use it. Take your chances with the homicidal housekeeper from hell. I'm sure she's less scary than me or the very benign ghost I'm about to call. It's not like I'm the one with the gun or anything."

A mountain of pain and regret fell away, leaving me with nothing except crystallized fury. "But do me a favor, would you? If she kills you, could you please just go into the light? I don't need another ghost hanging around. Two in one month is more than enough." I called Davina's name.

When fingers pinched my arm hard, I yelped. "What did you do that for? Are you trying to make sure we both end up dead?"

"Are you always this cranky when you're chasing a murderer?" Even whispered, it was the first time Neena had sounded like herself since I popped out of the ghost-seeing closet several weeks before.

"Today is an exception." I heard a noise, hissed for Neena to be quiet, and froze.

"Housekeeping," Nanette singsonged in a cheerful tone from the floor below.

"She's seriously not cleaning rooms right now," Neena leaned close to whisper.

"Not unless a gun cleans better than a broom. Now, hush!" Since she'd pinched me before, I felt entirely justified in returning the favor. "But if anything happens, I want you to keep crawling the way we came in. Go until you hit what feels like a dead end. It won't be, and you'll need to bear left. Follow that to the next dead end, and then go right. You'll hit the back of the closet in David's office, where there's another loose panel. There's a phone. You can call for help."

"You're not going after her without me."

"I will if there's a chance to take her down. You stay safe, and I'll send someone to get you when it's over, and then, you never have to see me again."

Maybe I'd sell the house and move. Make

it easier on everyone.

When the chill of death rolled over my skin, I knew Neena was about to live out her worst nightmare.

"You won't like what's about to happen, Neena, but if you freak out, we're both dead, so don't freak out. Davina, I'm not alone. You'll need to make the effort."

When Davina appeared, she brought a hint of light with her—enough that we could see her clearly, anyway. Neena sucked in a breath, but that was the only sound she made other than a slight scrabbling noise as she curled into herself to keep from touching any part of the ghost.

"What's the plan?" Davina wanted to know.

"You're looking at it. We're hiding until help shows up, which is where you come in. Go tell Leandra to call Ernie. Tell her to tell him to be careful because Nanette's got a gun, and she's already killed twice."

"I could do that." Davina's smile chilled me more than her touch did. "Or, I could get back a little of my own."

Neena slapped a hand over her mouth to muffle the squeal when Delilah's head popped through the panel. "Me, too."

My mind raced through possibilities.

"Let's play both sides of this thing, then. Go get Leandra to make the call, and then we'll see what we can do to keep Ernie from walking into a hail of gunfire, okay?"

Too cheerful for the situation, Davina grinned, faded away, then popped back to say, "Don't do anything fun while I'm gone."

"Fun?" Neena's voice came from the corner that had gone dark again once

Davina and Delilah were gone. "She's worse than the gun-toting whackjob that's chasing us. How do you do this?"

I knew what she meant, and there was no simple answer. "I have rules."

"For them or for you?"

"Them. They're basic and mostly have to do with privacy, as I feel I'm entitled to mine. So no ghosts in the bedroom or bathroom. No talking to me in public—that one's hard for them because they're not used to being dead. In addition to the privacy rules, I don't give messages to loved ones."

"I guess I figured that one out for myself." Neena's voice went cold, which is hard to pull off when you're whispering.

Had we finally come to the crux of the problem between us?

"Are you upset that I didn't tell you about

Hudson? Because your response to learning about Davina has been so balanced and thoughtful." I guessed we could both be cold when we wanted to, and I carried more bitterness than I thought. "I'm sorry."

"Sorry for what?" Neena's voice rose to a dangerous level.

"Shh."

"You're sorry you didn't offer me the solace of my husband's final words? Or sorry I found out you could have."

"But here's the thing, I did give you the message. I just didn't tell you where it came from. He said he loved you and wanted you to be happy. I did tell you both of those things when we first met, so you've had your message, and now you know it. I'll get you safely through today, and you can go back to pretending I'm the boogeyman if that's what it takes to make you feel better."

Whatever else she might have said got lost when Davina popped back from her mission.

"Ernie's on the way. Gonna be a few minutes. What's the plan?"

"Well, I'd like to come out of this one without a trip to the ER if that's okay with you. I'm pretty sure I could hold my own in hand to hand, but she's got a gun, and that changes things. Plus, she knows the inn almost as well as I do. We're safe here, but this hidey-hole is our only advantage."

"It's not your only advantage," Davina said. "You keep forgetting about me. What if I put the gun on ice?"

My knowledge of guns didn't extend much past the fact that they were mostly made of metal and were dangerous. "I have no idea if that would do any good or not."

"Not really," Neena offered. "Guns will fire in freezing weather and underwater."

In the ambient light of Davina's ghost, Neena caught my shocked look and shrugged. "My daddy likes to hunt. I know a few things about firearms."

"You and Patrea should start a club," I said, since Patrea also knew about guns.

"How cold are we talkin'?"

Ignoring how she flinched back, Davina trailed a finger down the string to Neena's hoodie. "That cold." She waited patiently while Neena tested the results. The string had gone stiff as a board.

"Can all ghosts do that?" Neena looked Davina in the face for the first time. "With just a touch?"

"I don't know about all ghosts, but I've had some practice."

"I can't," Delilah piped up. "I don't think, but then, I'm new."

"Doesn't matter," I cut in before we got too far off-topic. "What matters is if Davina can do anything to take the gun out of the picture. Preferably before Nanette finds us or Ernie walks into this mess and gets shot."

A few seconds passed in speculation before Neena relaxed enough to settle into a cross-legged position. "I need to know if she's carrying a pistol or a revolver, and it wouldn't hurt to have someone keeping track of her movements."

From the noises echoing through the empty inn, Nanette was still a floor below us, searching through the guest rooms. We didn't have a lot of time.

"I'll volunteer to keep an eye on her, but I don't know anything about guns." Delilah offered.

Davina shrugged. "I guess I know a little bit. Enough to tell the difference between a pistol and a revolver, anyway. I'll go take a look." She popped out and was only gone a few seconds. "Revolver. On the smaller side, I think. Like maybe it's a woman's weapon."

"Probably a .22 then," Neena decided. "Still deadly, but I think we can work with the freeze-ray thing."

"Nice mental image of Davina shooting ice out of her finger, but it doesn't work exactly like that."

Neena flapped a hand at me, then turned back to Davina.

"You'll need to go for the hammer if you

want to disable the gun entirely.”

Davina frowned. “Not the trigger?”

“A good second option if you have enough juice, but the gun is useless if the hammer can’t make contact with the round.”

“Okay,” Davina nodded. “Just so I’m clear, the hammer is on top, the bit she pulls back before firing, right?”

Neena nodded. “Jam it up good and tight. That should give the solid folk at least a couple of minutes to take her down.”

“We’ll have to be ready.” We were already in the best place to mount our attack if we could get her into the right spot. Or rather, my attack since I intended to get Neena as far out of the way as possible before anything went down. “Delilah, how do you feel about becoming bait? I need you to lure Nanette into the right position for an ambush."

"Can do. We'll go size up the situation. Be right back."

Leaving me alone with Neena, both ghosts faded temporarily.

"They're gone," I said, running over the plan one more time in my head.

"I have eyes, don't I?"

So much for staving off a tension headache. Pain bloomed behind my eyes.

"If things go south, this could be your last chance, so why don't you just say whatever you want to say to me?" I'd had all of the situation I could take.

"How many times?"

Several possible answers popped into my head, but since I wasn't sure what she meant, I didn't let any of them out. "How many times what?"

"Hudson. How many times was he with me, and you never said a word? How many times did he ask you to break your rule for me, and you didn't?"

Oh, jeez. I should have realized she'd jump to that conclusion and be hurt. Because I needed a second, I rubbed my forehead. Not that she could see me since Davina had taken the ambient lighting with her when she went.

"Only twice."

Her intake of breath told me I'd missed the mark if I'd meant to reassure.

"He asked me to tell you he loved you, and I did. Maybe I didn't say the message came from him, but I did give it to you. In my own way."

"Whatever."

"Okay, fine." I'd hit my limit with her. "You

want to know everything? Fine. Here you go. He hit on me before he was killed. Not because he was interested in me but because he was using stupid logic. He was hurt that you thought he'd cheated. I turned him down cold, by the way. And then, after he died, he asked me to make friends with you for his sake. To keep an eye on you, to help you get through his death. He said I owed him a favor because of our history. Does that make you feel better to hear?"

"No," Neena's voice sounded funny. A moment later, I heard what sounded like a sob, but I didn't dare to reach out.

"I'm sorry. I realize I bungled the whole thing, but he was my first ghost. It's not like I had a history of experience, let alone a clue about what I was doing. I wanted to be friends with you because you're awesome, not because of any favor, which by the way, I didn't owe him. Or not at the time." I'd hit the rambling phase of the conversation. Great.

Another choked sound. Only this time, I didn't think it sounded like crying.

"Are you laughing right now?"

I felt a hand on my arm, and I felt Neena's body shake through that contact.

"I loved my husband, but he was an absolute idiot."

Like I was dumb enough to agree with her. Except I did. "He was. Maybe. A little. I do think his feelings for you were genuine. What he did, he did for love."

"Oh, I know that. Hudson was a good man, but he'd have taken home the gold if jumping to conclusions was an actual sport."

"He saved my life, you know, so I probably

do owe him that favor."

Neena sidled closer, so we sat beside each other, our sides touching. Maybe there was hope for us after all.

"Just so you know," I turned to her in the dark. "I was never friends with you because he told me I should be. I like you. You're one of my favorite people, and I've missed you."

"God, Ev. Me, too. It's been horrible, and I should have known you weren't holding out on me out of spite."

"Then can I offer you the silver medal for conclusion jumping, and can we just be over it, now? Or can you not handle the ghosts at all? Because Davina says she can make my ability go away or become dormant. Something about closing a door to keep them out. Whatever it is, she's going to try."

Sucking in an audible breath, Neena grabbed for me in the dark and got hold of my wrist. "Not on my account, please. I would feel just horrible if you couldn't help dead people because of me, and you're gonna have to accept the bronze if you thought it was your ability I couldn't handle."

"I haven't decided anything yet. But I've been thinking about the future a lot."

Davina interrupted girl talk time.

"She's on her way up here. You have maybe two minutes. What's the plan?"

There hadn't been time for a complicated plan, and simple is always better, anyway. If Delilah maneuvered Nanette into place, and Davina managed to disable the gun, and I could take her from behind, that would leave Neena free to circle around to David's office. She'd be our last line of defense and cut off

Nanette's only escape route if I couldn't restrain her.

Ernie was coming, so we only had to keep the gun out of play and not let Nanette get away. Should be easy enough for two flesh and bloods and a couple of spectral figures. Or one flesh and blood if I had my way.

"Just make sure she's not too close to this panel, and get her to face away from it," I whispered to Delilah as we heard Nanette's feet on the stairs. "Neena, go now. Quiet as a mouse."

For once, I had the drop on the bad guy, and I intended to keep it that way. A surge of adrenaline made my scalp tingle as I heard the soft shuffling of Neena's knees on the boards and Nanette's taunting voice in the hallway. It was almost go-time when I realized there was a flaw in the plan. We should have come up with a codeword, so I'd know when to make my move.

It couldn't be helped now, so I pressed my ear against the panel and listened as Delilah took a little license so she could get some of her own back. If silence hadn't been the word of the moment, I might have been tempted to break into applause when her voice rose in spooky tones.

"Nanette Hill. Turn and face your doom."

Okay, so maybe I was tempted to break into a fit of the giggles. Either way, go, Delilah!

Then a gunshot sounded, and things weren't so funny anymore.

"Missed me," Delilah taunted. "Want to try again?"

Two more bullets hit the wall. David wasn't going to be happy about that. How many shots did she have? Neena might have known, but I'd sent her away.

"Get back," Nanette shouted, but from too close. It sounded like she was blocking the panel. Not helpful. "You're not real."

"Sure I am. Why don't you come and see for yourself?"

Nanette might not hear Delilah's desperation, but I did. This whole plan depended on her getting Nanette into the right position, and she was failing at the first hurdle.

"Come on, Delilah, you got this," I whispered, but Delilah couldn't hear me.

"She's blowing it," Davina popped her head through the panel. "And your cop friend is outside. We don't have much time."

None is what we had because Ernie announced himself. I guessed I should have told Davina to tell Leandra to tell him to use stealth mode. Too late now.

"Boo." When Delilah's voice sounded to my right and Davina's head disappeared, I figured they'd worked it out. Nanette moved away from the ghostly echo, and when another came, I heard her turn. It was now or never.

Gently, I pushed the bottom of the panel open and peered out to see Nanette right where I wanted her. Moving like a ghost myself, I oozed out of the hidden space and rose up behind Nanette, whose attention was firmly focused on Delilah.

Davina took her cue, laid a finger on the gun, and squeezed her eyes shut to concentrate. A rime of frost appeared on the metal, spreading outward from the hammer down the barrel and into the grip.

"What the—" Nanette's attention wavered from Delilah as the gun went too cold to handle. Okay, well, that hadn't been the plan exactly, but it worked a treat. Out of reflex, Nanette tossed the gun away and looked at fingers blue with cold.

I took my cue and jumped her from behind. Delilah gave one valiant effort, zipped in close, and jammed a fist right in Nanette's face. I felt the chill of it since mine wasn't that far away, then her energy depleted, and Delilah phased out. Davina was already gone, and with Neena safely out of the way, it came down to just Nanette and me. Exactly how I wanted it.

Quickly regaining her composure, Nanette drove her elbow back, connecting with my cheekbone. Pain flared quick and hot as she spun out of my grip. She let her center of gravity go low, raised her fists, and took a stance.

"I've done a little boxing in my time," Nanette bragged.

Not enough, I thought when she danced forward, jabbed twice, and totally telegraphed her intention. I dodged the blows, then partially scored with an uppercut she didn't quite manage to avoid. My fist glanced off her chin with not quite enough force.

"My boyfriend teaches self-defense. I'm his star pupil." At least it was half true. Maybe more than half. I'd never asked. With the gun still on the floor nearby, my only plan was to keep her from getting close enough to grab it while I waited for Ernie to show up. Seemed like it was taking him forever, but time tends to become elastic during moments of great tension.

And so, we danced for a moment, and I returned the favor to Nanette's cheekbone when I nailed her with a roundhouse kick. She went down but came back up, shaking her head.

"Good one." Her eyes glittered like ice as she glanced toward the gun, estimated her chances, then decided to go for it.

I beat her there, but barely, and kicked the gun down the hallway. Or that was the intention, anyway. It probably would have worked better if the carpet hadn't provided enough friction to reduce the gun's forward motion. The moment of distraction cost me a black eye as Nanette's fist connected, and I staggered back.

Adrenaline sped my heartbeat, turning it into a metronome.

Nanette thought to take advantage of my distraction and dodged in for another punch intended to disable me so she could get to the gun, but I ducked and, when she went off balance, returned the favor of a black eye.

We sized each other up for a moment, then both of us went for the gun at once. My hand closed on bare metal that wasn't nearly cold enough anymore. Nanette's hand viced on my wrist, her thumb jamming into the tendons to make me let go. She suffered an elbow in the gut for her efforts, but as the pain bent her double, her finger slid into the trigger ring, and she gave it a yank.

"I've got you now," came her triumphant cry.

"The hell you do." Neena burst out of the

panel behind Nanette, shot a straight-armed punch to the side of her head, and followed through with an impressive kick to the wrist of the hand holding the gun.

Blam. The gun went off.

White hot pain seared across my bicep. Neena shrieked. Nanette regained her grip on the weapon.

"Why?" Blood dripped down my arm, but I didn't look to see how bad it was. The adrenaline kept me on my feet as I faced down the barrel of the weapon. "At least give me that much before you shoot me."

"Why? Because you're trying to get me arrested." Maybe Nanette wasn't that bright.

"No. Why did you kill Davina?"

"Because she was a meddling bitch. My uncle, the only person in my life that actually ever gave a damn, got me out, and she came along and sent me right back to the living hell of my father's bed."

Recharged enough to show herself, the ghost in question popped up next to me but was so faint I could see right through her. She wouldn't be freezing the gun a second time. "I didn't know." Sorrow coated her words. "Her father seemed genuinely concerned. He was inconsolable at the loss, and I thought the uncle was the bad guy."

"I'm sure she didn't know what was going on. You have to consider how things looked from the outside. It wasn't her fault."

"Doesn't matter, now, does it? She put me back there, took away the only person who ever treated me with kindness, and gave my father enough sympathetic press that no one would believe me if I told them what he'd been doing to me. As if they would anyway. My mother didn't."

"I'm sorry for what happened to you, but what did Delilah ever do to you?"

"She recognized me, and she's a talker, so she had to go."

"I did?" Delilah's voice came from nowhere. "I don't remember that."

To stall, I asked the next question that had been bothering me. "Why did you wait so many years to go after Davina? That's what I don't understand."

Her face going hard, Nanette shrugged. "My father was dying. No great loss. I planned to dance on his grave. After years of therapy, I thought I'd let it all go until a couple of months back when I found out the old bastard put her in his will as a thank-you for finding me. The way I see it, her getting a million dollars for sending me back to that hellhole was like her becoming my pimp. She sold me back to him. Turned me into a whore. I'm nobody's whore."

Anyone could see the pain on Nanette's face. Didn't excuse her actions, but I did feel bad for her. Not a lot since she didn't seem to care if I lived or died, but some.

"I'm sorry. Tell her I'm sorry," Davina implored, knowing the request went against my rules for dealing with the dead. "Please."

I shrugged. This probably wasn't the time for that, but who knew? Maybe it would distract Nanette long enough for Ernie to haul his butt up the stairs. He should have been here by now.

"I, uh, I don't quite know how to say this, but I see ghosts, and you should know that Davina's here right now, and she says she's sorry."

Even though I knew it was coming, it hurt when Nanette looked at me like I'd either grown horns or wasn't all there.

"Believe me or don't. I'm just passing on the message. Which goes against my rules, but whatever."

She must have believed a little because Nanette glanced around in case she could see Davina, and I took the opportunity to advance a step in her direction. From behind, Neena did the same. I caught her eye and narrowed mine in an attempt to tell her to stand down.

"Screw her. And screw you, too." The gun had dipped just a fraction but came up again when she focused her full attention on me. "You're a meddling pain in the ass, but I will feel bad when you're gone. Just a little. I kind of liked you."

"I'm not gone yet." For the second time in my life, I followed Drew and Riley's training. Moving as quickly as possible, I raised the palm of my good arm, slammed it into the gun's barrel, and took Nanette by surprise. The weapon flew out of her hand, and when she fumbled to try and catch it, Neena stepped up and rammed her elbow into the side of her head.

"That's for shooting my friend." Neena followed up with a solid punch to the chin. Nanette's eyes rolled back, and she dropped just as Ernie huffed to a stop at the top of the stairs.

"Everyone okay?" He wasted no time slapping the cuffs on Nanette.

"Not exactly." I wavered.

"That bitch shot Everly." Neena raced to my side, gingerly touched my arm. "Come on, honey, you need to sit down."

"I think it's just a flesh wound." But the adrenaline leaking out of my system made me shaky. "The bullet grazed my arm. Could have been worse. What took you so long?"

Ernie shrugged and had the decency to look sorry. "You were doing such a good job of getting a confession out of her, I had to wait until you got it all." He pointed to his recorder. "Makes the case easier. I didn't think she'd shoot you."

"About that," Neena glared at Ernie, "We need to get Everly to the hospital."

"I'm okay. A little shaky, though, and I guess I'll need a couple of stitches."

"Paramedics are already here. I told them to come in quiet."

The forethought went some way to earning Neena's forgiveness. "I'll go tell them to get up here." She left me alone with Ernie and Nanette.

"About that ghost thing," Ernie said. "Truth or just buying time?"

I cocked an eyebrow at him, "What do you think?"

CHAPTER TWENTY-ONE

A round of patching up at the hospital proved the injury looked worse than it was. A few stitches and painkillers later, Drew showed up at the hospital with my parents in tow. Worry and fear worked itself out through tears and recriminations.

"Can we talk about the details later?" I gave a quick nod to indicate the technician who'd come in to remove the IV from my arm. He didn't need to hear the story, given it was full of ghostly content. "I'm a little banged up, but I'm okay, and that's all that matters."

"She was brilliant." Neena had ridden with me in the ambulance and, other than during the actual stitching-up part hadn't left my side since we arrived. When she'd returned, her skinned knuckles sported bandages and an ice pack, so I figured she'd taken the time to get herself fixed up a bit, too.

"Me? What about you? All I did was disarm her and get myself shot in the process. You're the one who took Nanette down. You'd have been proud of her, Drew. She clocked that bitch good and proper." The pain medication seemed to have loosened my tongue, but for once, my mother didn't lecture me on the inappropriate uses of the word *bitch*.

Eyebrows shooting up, Neena protested. "All you did? Are you freaking kidding me right now? She'd have shot Ernie before he realized she had a gun. You probably saved his life and mine, too."

"I didn't do it alone." The comment was meant for Neena, and she knew exactly what I meant by it. Davina had played a pivotal role in the capture of her killer.

"You're right. I owe her a debt of gratitude as well."

"We'll talk about all of that later." Her face having regained most of its color, Kitty Dupree did what she did best: she took charge. "Did I hear them say you were being released?"

I nodded. "It was just a flesh wound, which I think is a weird term. You don't hear people talking about bone wounds or muscle wounds. And you certainly don't leave the hairdresser thinking you'd had a hair wound." The medicated squirrel began to chase his tail in my head. "Oh, but you do hear about the occasional head wound, but never a foot or hand wound."

"She's babbling. Are you sure she didn't hit her head?" My dad turned to Neena, who shook hers.

"I'm fine, dad. I feel really good right now." It was definitely the medication talking. That is the only excuse I have for ordering Drew to take me home and take me to bed.

He leaned down, kissed my forehead, and offered my parents a quirked smile. "I'll take you home and put you to bed. How's that?"

"You're no fun."

I fell asleep in the car, so Drew followed through on his promise. I vaguely remember him waking me once to take more painkillers, and other than some soreness woke up feeling fairly decent the next morning. That feeling lasted right up until I noticed Davina and Delilah sitting on the end of the bed.

"Guess that's that, eh?" Davina said. "I never suspected her for a minute, but then, I wouldn't have, I suppose."

"Nor, me," Delilah added.

But in a bout of armchair quarterbacking, I thought maybe I should have. "She smelled of carnations from that cleaner, and I didn't make the connection until it was almost too late. Delilah was a big help in solving this one."

Delilah preened a little at the praise while Davina's mouth firmed into a line, but only for a second or two. "You're right. Delilah, I owe you an apology. We could have become true friends if I'd trusted you more."

Preening even more, Delilah lit right up.

Except she didn't, actually.

"Hey, what's that?" Delilah turned her face to the right, where an invisible light cast a glow across her cheekbones.

"It's time," I said. "You can cross over now. Go into the light. I don't know what you'll find there, but I feel it's good. Can't you?"

Maybe it was the quality of the light or that whatever was on the other side filled her with serenity, but when Delilah smiled, her face shone with goodness. "I guess you're right. I'm ready for my next adventure. I'm sure we'll meet again sometime. Until then, be careful."

Delilah went into the light without so much as a backward glance, but with promises yet to keep, Davina stayed behind, and after a moment, the light faded.

"Godspeed," Davina said, and then she also faded. She wasn't the only one with promises to keep, and I'd need to set up a meeting with Jason, but first, I needed the bathroom.

Drew came in just as I walked back into the bedroom.

"How are you feeling? Do you need help?" His eyes filled with concern, and he brushed my cheek with his fingers and offered a gentle kiss.

"Not too bad. Delilah just left."

"Like left left, or just went away for a while."

"She crossed over."

"Davina?"

"I'm still here." She popped into his line of sight, and he didn't even miss a beat. You have to love a man who can adapt to your freaky friends. "We have unfinished business before I go."

"More than you know," I admitted. "Davina, we need to talk."

"Sounds ominous," she said.

"Sounds like something that could wait until after breakfast," Drew moved to my side. "Do you need any help getting dressed?"

"I don't think so, but thanks." I gave Davina a look, and when that didn't do the trick, flicked a finger toward the door. She took the hint and left.

"Nothing I haven't seen before," she muttered.

I picked out a soft sweater with loose sleeves, paired it with loose pants, and decided makeup could wait. The scents of sausage and coffee hit me in the face when

I opened the door, and my stomach growled.

Davina laughed with Drew in the kitchen while they waited for me to emerge.

"What's the joke?" I opened the cabinet where we kept the mugs, but Drew gently got in my way.

"I'll get it." He doctored a mug the way I liked it, then filled me a plate from the pans warming in the oven.

"You made waffles?" My stomach growled again. "You're the best."

"Don't get too excited. I used a boxed mix. They're not from scratch."

I loaded mine with butter and syrup, then cut off a bite. "You will not hear me complain." I dug in.

"I've already eaten, and it sounds like you two need to talk. I'll be downstairs if you need me," Drew dropped a kiss on the top of my head as he passed by.

With him gone, I tried to find the right words to tell Davina about Jason, then gave up and went for my laptop and the visual. Davina watched over my shoulder as I pulled up the image of the boy in his motorcycle and one of her from her high school years.

"Is that the father of your child?" I pointed to the boy, and Davina nodded. "Okay." I hit the button to run the simulation and waited for the spinning doodad to stop. When it did, I popped the resulting image into the age progression software while the air around me took in a decided chill.

I'd known this would freak her out. That's why I'd chosen a warm sweater.

"What's that? What are you doing? I don't

want to see this," she said.

"I know." I felt bad for her, but I'd promised my mother I'd handle the situation. Giving Davina the information and letting her decide seemed the right thing to do. Gently, I locked the selection box to the baby's face and moved the slider to the right. Tears welled as he aged, and I didn't need to get him to the adult stage to see the resemblance to Jason.

I'd have hugged her if I could because it looked like she needed comfort.

"We both do. It's Jason. He's your son, and he's been looking for you." I told her about Jason tracking his birth mother to Mooselick River. "He thought it was my mom for a little while. It broke her heart to dash his hopes."

"Does he know? About me, I mean."

I shook my head. "I wouldn't do that without speaking to you first. If you want to reconnect with him, I will help you do that. If you prefer to go into the light—or wherever it is you're planning to go—without giving Jason the gift of closure, that's also up to you."

Tentatively, Davina touched the computer screen. "My boy."

Rising, I rinsed my plate and stashed it in the dishwasher to give her a minute to think things through. When I returned to the table, she changed the subject.

"I've decided not to cross over. Not for a while, yet."

"You're going to stay behind to help others cross over." I'd seen it coming, and the unselfish side of me thought the plan a good one. The selfish part worried she planned to break her promise to me.

"I think I can do some good."

"Undoubtedly." I waited for whatever came next. We were both standing at a crossroads, wanting to go in different directions.

Davina stated the obvious. "You could help me."

"Or I could be normal again."

The air chilled. "I said I would handle it, and I will, but normal shouldn't be your goal. It isn't aspirational. It's a resting state at best. You have something extraordinary. Why would you give that up?"

I pointed to my sore arm. "Because this type of thing keeps happening. Because I want to marry that man downstairs and have babies with him. I don't want those babies to grow up in a house disrupted by ghosts. I don't want them to be like me."

Leaning back in her seat, Davina pinned me with a look. "You're an idiot."

"Excuse me?"

"Think about it for a minute. Giving up your ability won't stop your children from developing theirs. It's in your DNA."

I wanted to put my hands over my ears and drown her out with the La La, Can't Hear You song. Instead, I admitted, "You're probably right. Looks like we both have things to think about and decisions to make."

"I think I've made mine." Davina sounded both unsure and determined. An odd combination. "I'd like to meet my son."

When I went to the pot for a refill of coffee, she gave me a look.

"Oh, you mean right now."

Considering how the air had begun to vibrate around me, the sooner, the better, or things could get ugly.

"Before I chicken out." At least she was honest about her feelings, so I called down the stairs to tell Drew I was leaving.

"Do you really think this is the best time to go gallivanting all over town?" he yelled back.

"It's for a good reason."

"Gallivanting?" Davina huffed out a laugh as we heard Drew's feet on the stairs. "Who says that anymore?"

"If you're dead set on going, I'll drive." He didn't wait for me to agree but grabbed his coat and helped me into mine while Davina informed us she'd meet me there and faded. I used her absence as an excuse to explain the urgency to Drew.

"This could wait. You're injured."

"It's a scratch."

"A scratch from a bullet. That's no minor thing. It's a traumatic event."

Only an idiot would disagree. I could still hear the gunshot echo in my head, but only if things were quiet. Introducing Davina Benet to her biological son would not fall under the heading of quiet, which was fine with me. I needed the distraction, so I made him follow me to the car and let him fuss over buckling my seat belt.

I didn't talk much on the short drive to the inn. I was too busy trying to figure out what to say to Jason. *Hey, I can talk to ghosts, and your mother is one of them* seemed like the wrong way to go.

"I'm nervous," I admitted. Drew patted my knee as he pulled into the space nearest the door. "What if I say the wrong thing?"

"Speak from your heart. That way, whatever happens, you did your best." With that, Drew reached across me to open my door. "I'll wait here."

"Chicken." But I leaned in for a kiss and heard soft clucking noises as I closed the car door behind me.

David sat behind the counter, his head in his hands.

Uh oh.

"Hey, everything okay?"

His head came up, and his eyes locked on my face. "Never mind me. Are you okay?"

"It looked a lot worse than it was. Sorry about the bullet holes in the walls. Things got out of hand there for a few minutes."

"Out of hand?" David rose, circled the desk, and would have grabbed me by the arms to make a point, but I stepped back. "You were shot by someone I hired to work here. I hired a killer, and she nearly murdered someone I care about. Do you have any idea how that makes me feel?"

Looked like I had a few more fires to put out than merely getting Jason and Davina together.

"Nanette had us all fooled, David. You can't blame yourself for her actions. I certainly don't blame you for anything that happened. Nanette is right where she belongs. In jail. No one else was hurt or killed, and I escaped with nothing more than a few stitches."

My demeanor got through to him, and since he'd calmed, I asked if Jason was in the kitchen. "I need to speak with him in private."

Going back to his perch behind the tall desk, David waved a hand toward the rear of the inn. "Ernie was in here early this morning and cleared us to open. We have guests coming in later, so Jason's cooking. Miranda agreed to fill in until I can find someone permanent, so I guess we're back to normal. She's up there now, with a big bottle of peroxide, cleaning your blood off the hall carpet."

I shuddered and decided I didn't need to go upstairs for anything.

"Thanks. I'll go and speak to Jason, then." I turned back. "And don't forget, it's game night on Saturday. I'll expect you by seven."

CHAPTER TWENTY-TWO

"Try this." I'd barely walked through the door when Jason handed me a plate. Davina stood near the stove, her face white from the strain of the situation.

Out of reflex more than interest, I took a bite of what looked like a dark fudge brownie wrapped around a peanut butter cookie. I might have groaned a little it was so good.

"Sinful," I pronounced.

"Do you think it needs nuts?"

"Sure." I couldn't concentrate on the nuts

or no nuts question. "Jason, can we talk for a minute? There's something I need to tell you."

Grinning, he glanced at me. "My ploy of feeding you finally worked, and you're leaving Drew for me? I knew it was only a matter of time."

He made me smile. "No, but tempting. Anyway, you spoke to my mother recently."

The smile fell off his face.

"She told you." Not a question.

"She did, and while she was sorry to disappoint you…this is harder than I thought it would be…she didn't tell you the full truth."

Hope flared in his eyes.

"My mother isn't your mother, but Lucy Bennett probably was."

"Lucy Bennett?" Jason pulled out a stool and sat as if he didn't trust his legs to hold him.

"You'd know her better by her stage name. Lucy Bennett is, or was, Davina Benet." In as few words as possible, I told him the whole story while Davina waited nearby.

"Davina Benet. I never thought…I mean…I didn't get to meet her when she was here. And now that she's gone, I never will." The man looked like a whipped puppy. Even if I'd briefly considered not telling him about my ability, I couldn't let the moment pass. The trouble was I needed a good way to broach the subject.

Should I blurt out my truth? Or should I try to ease him in slowly?

"I'm here now." Davina took the decision out of my hands by appearing to her son.

Jason put a hand down on the stainless steel table where he rolled out pie crusts, his face went pale, and I could see the pulse in his throat jumping.

"You could have given me a minute to ease him into things." I turned a stern look in Davina's direction.

"You can see her, too?"

"Yes, I can." I still wasn't happy with her. "I brought her here to meet you, but she was supposed to wait until I had time to explain." I turned to Jason. "I see ghosts. Or, if you want to get technical about it, they haunt me until I help them cross over. Davina here, she should have crossed over once we solved her murder, but she decided to hang around a while longer and meet her son."

"Okay." Jason swallowed hard. "I guess I'm glad to meet you." His gaze kept sliding in her direction and then away. This couldn't be easy for him.

"I'm sure you have questions, and you should know Davina can only remain visible for a short while. It takes a lot of energy for her to show herself. She has more than most, but I'd say you have no more than half an hour with her. I'll leave the two of you to get acquainted in private."

An awkward silence followed me out of the room.

"Everything okay?" David asked when I returned to the reception area. Once, I'd have automatically brushed him off, but since he knew my ghostly secret, I saw no need for that.

"Jason's adopted. He moved here because he'd tracked his birth mother to Mooselick River, but it turns out she was murdered before he had a chance to meet her, so I've brought her here to rectify the oversight."

It never occurred to me that David would see a problem with that plan.

"Great. I'm short a housekeeper, and now, you want to take my breakfast chef away, too."

"Where did you get that idea from?"

A loud crack sounded when David slapped a hand on the desktop. "If he only came here to find his mother, don't you think he'll move on once he has?"

I hadn't, but now, I did.

"Oh. Sorry. I guess I didn't look at it like that. Bringing Davina here seemed like the right thing to do."

Resigned, David ran a hand through already ruffled hair. "It was the right thing for him. I can't fault your logic, but I hope it doesn't cost me a chef. Maybe I can talk the folks at the new bakery into supplying the inn with pastries for a few months while I look for someone else."

"You might be wrong about Jason. He seems to be settling in here. He might decide to stay on if you offered him free rein in the food area. You know he talked about expanding the menu when you hired him on. You could have a nice little boutique eating establishment on your hands."

I speculated, leaning back to glance at the small dining room. "Fancy linens and place settings, keep it to three or four tables, so it feels more exclusive. You'll get more honeymooners and anniversary guests if you provide them with a singular experience. I can help you with the advertising."

I could see it in my head: the table, the

candlelight gleaming off of sparkling crystal, and Jason's food shown to perfection. An ad like that would sell the heck out of the inn. David must have seen a glimmer of hope when I described my vision.

"Okay, all of that sounds great. I'll keep that plan in my back pocket and drag it out if I get the impression he's decided to ditch me."

Since David was receptive, I killed time by tossing out a few more of the ideas I'd been keeping in reserve—the ones I judged he was ready to hear, anyway. I had plenty more but didn't want to overwhelm him with the scope of them.

Davina walked through the kitchen door—quite literally—about ten minutes later. "I need you."

"I guess we'll finish this later," I said to

David.

His response earned him a mock glare. "Have fun."

Back in the kitchen, Davina had gone transparent around the edges. It wouldn't be long before she faded entirely. "What can I do for you?"

"I'm sorry," was all she said before I felt the unmistakable sensation of her ghostly chill spreading through my body as she took it over without asking. "I need to hug my son." That last sounded only in my head.

"I'd have let you if you asked, but this is highly rude," I thought at her as my body moved forward to hug Jason without my intention behind the motion. Being possessed by a ghost feels like those dreams where you're frozen, but things are happening all around you. It's weird, and I don't care for it one bit.

Except that Davina's emotions translated to me in a surge of unexpected joy followed by an equal measure of sorrow. Maybe this was too little, too late, but it was all I could do for her as Jason cried in my/her arms, and she used my mouth to murmur comforting words in his ear.

Meanwhile, in my head, I recited poetry to avoid feeling like an interloper, which was why I missed it when Davina said goodbye to her son, then pulled back to do for me what she'd promised.

"It's time," her voice vibrated like a gong on the inside of my skull. Another fun perk of this ghostly lifestyle no one told me about. Not that anyone told me anything. Ghosts are so ungrateful.

"You sure you want me to do this? There's

no going back if you go through with it."

She didn't sound entirely certain of that fact.

My ears rang. Probably a sign of a spike in blood pressure. A hazy mist fell over my vision, obscuring everything in gray softness.

"What," I asked, "are you doing in there?"

It felt like she was a library patron, and I was the card catalog that held the secrets to finding her favorite book as she took me apart and put me back together in a slightly different configuration.

"Are you done yet?" As life-changing events went, this one was shaping up as the weirdest in recent months.

"No, I'm not done."

Crabbiness. From Davina. Shocking.

I heard her mumble something right before

a resounding click echoed from deep inside. Pieces of my essence or soul or whatever word would best describe the ineffable thing that made me Everly flew apart, spun wildly, and tried to fit back into the whole.

It's working, I thought, forgetting Davina could hear my thoughts.

"Almost," she said. "I just have to—"

I don't know what her next words would have been because she screamed, the sound turning my insides into one long, taut, quivering wire that vibrated me to pieces. And then we melded together in a way that's hard to explain. For a moment, I was Davina, and she was me.

My knees wobbled, so I reached for the closest solid item—the table—to stay upright. My hand brushed against Jason's mixing bowl, and a series of images of him whisking and mixing flooded my mind. Was this how Davina's talent worked?

Blinding light flared as Davina was dragged away from me by force. Out of instinct, she grabbed on to try and finish the job, but I knew it was over. Davina was going into the light whether she wanted to or not.

A thousand bees buzzed in my ears as a curtain fell, and my world went dark.

Hours or seconds passed. Time had no meaning, and what did it matter anyway? Davina had been inside me when she crossed over. She'd killed me. Or worse.

Was there something worse? I wasn't sure.

I drifted through endless night, wondering why I couldn't see the light until a sound penetrated the darkness.

"Hello, my darling girl."

I recognized a voice I never expected to hear again.

"Grammie Dupree?"

-The End-